PR...

Anab...

NOTTING HILL MYSTERIES

An Uncommon Murder

'A book to gulp down in one sitting . . . The sparkling
writing and immediacy of the characterization plus
a gripping mystery raise this well above the
average detective novel.'
Sunday Telegraph

'One of my top ten crime novels for 1992.'
Scotland on Sunday

In at the Deep End

'A fizzy entertainment . . . done with a skill and
velocity that demands a second helping.'
Matthew Coady, *Guardian*

'More please! And more!'
Christopher Wordsworth, *Observer*

'Ms Donald lines up the suspects with all the skill
of a sergeant-major on the parade ground.'
Stephen Walsh, *Oxford Times*

The Glass Ceiling

'Donald is an inventive writer, with prose as
sparkly as a string of diamonds.'
Oxford Times

'A powerful sense of place, bringing the
London of the nineties vividly to life in
this fast, absorbing read.'
Val McDermid

'Thrillerish, prodigiously lively crime
novel . . . Most engaging.'
Literary Review

The Loop

'An intriguing mixture of wry humour, low-life sleaze
and cult religion, interspersed with the saga of its
heroine's hopeless love life. Perfect for the beach.'
Cosmopolitan

'A young, fun beach read featuring Alex Tanner,
likable and feisty TV researcher and sometime
private eye.'
Paisley Daily Express

The Loop

Born in India and educated at a convent boarding school and Oxford, Anabel Donald has been writing fiction since 1982 when her first novel, *Hannah at Thirty-five*, was published to great critical acclaim. She has worked as a lecturer and for many years was headmistress at a school in Doncaster. Anabel is currently fulfilling her long-held ambition to journey across America by Harley-Davidson motorbike.

There are now five novels in the Notting Hill Mysteries series, of which *The Loop* is the fourth. The most recent novel, *Destroy Unopened*, is just published in Pan paperback.

Also in this series

Anabel Donald

The Loop

PAN BOOKS

For Miles Donald
il miglior fabbro
and a very funny man

First published 1996 by Macmillan

This edition published 1997 by Pan Books
an imprint of Macmillan Publishers Ltd
25 Eccleston Place, London SW1W 9NF
Basingstoke and Oxford

Associated companies throughout the world

ISBN 0 330 34784 5

A CIP catalogue record for this book is available from
the British Library

Phototypeset by Intype London Ltd
Printed by Mackays of Chatham PLC, Chatham, Kent

Sunday, 27 March

Chapter One

My row with Barty finally erupted over Newfoundland.

Or Labrador.

I still don't know which, and I don't want to know, though I suspect he was right. I'll check when I can bear to.

We were nearly seven hours out on the British Airways flight from Heathrow, not far from our destination, Chicago. We were in First Class and I had the window seat and Barty'd been silent for at least three hours, which was a relief, though he'd been snoring, which wasn't.

For the first few hours I'd thought I was in freebie heaven and I'd mopped up everything. Six little bottles of champagne (three of them Barty's), the dinner (I had appetizers, soup, lobster, steak, and cheese), five cups of coffee, three mineral waters and the complimentary slippers (stupid name: when were you last flattered by a slipper?). I'd also been to the loo three times and plundered the courtesy toiletries, male and female (I could always use the aftershave on my legs and armpits).

Then Barty'd told me that in First Class they'd give you more or less anything you asked for, which spoilt my fun completely. That meant I wasn't being a sharp-witted scavenger, just a bloated greedhead.

So I'd sulked and watched two films on my individual fold-up screen, the second while Barty slept. I was too excited to sleep; I didn't want to miss a second of the flight. I love aeroplanes, and I was thinking about America. I'd only ever been to America in my dreams.

The hostess turned up with the snack suppers. I nudged Barty and put his table down. He half woke, grunted, and waved his food away. I waved it right back.

When the hostess had gone he peered at me and said, 'I don't eat much on aeroplanes.'

He'd told me that several times already, along with the rest of his frequent-flyer information like 'alcohol dehydrates you' and 'don't take your boots off, your feet will swell up and you won't be able to get them on again.'

'I eat tons on aeroplanes,' I said.

He didn't point out I could ask for more food of my own. Instead, 'OK,' he said peaceably, which was infuriating in itself. 'Where are we?'

I looked out and down to the pack ice on the frozen sea beneath us. Or perhaps it was the snow on the frozen land. It was beautiful, either way.

'Newfoundland, I think.'

'Can't be,' he said. 'It must be Labrador.'

And that was when I stuffed the complimentary slippers in his mouth.

He took it well. He takes everything well. But I didn't think he understood it, which was surprising because he's usually intuitive and quick.

But he should have known – we'd been lovers for over four months. He's an independent television producer and I'd worked for him for years, on and off, as a researcher. He knows my work habits: solitary and quick. He knows my personal habits: autonomous. He knows that America is my magic country, and that I'd never been there.

Considering all that information, for the past week he'd been behaving like the rear end of a pantomime horse.

The trouble began when Alan Protheroe offered me three days' work in Chicago setting up interviews and locations for a drugs documentary. I jumped at it, particularly since Alan's idea of three days' work could be completed by a normal human being in one. I booked the return ticket (economy) and the hotel (chosen by Alan). Both of these would be covered by expenses.

Then I'd bought a Delta Airlines five-flight pass, and paid for it with my own money. When I'd wrapped up the research I'd fly around America. I'd walk the streets of San Francisco and Los Angeles and Boston and think of the fictional private detectives, my heroes, who had walked them before me.

OK, it was juvenile, but without those private eyes my childhood would have been lonely, perhaps even unendurable. They'd kept me going. When I'd first started to read them I'd been seven and none too clear about my sexual identity. I was a tomboy who had to be bullied into a dress (ever tried to climb in a dress?), my name was Alex, and I had cropped hair – because I nearly always had lice and each new set of foster-parents thought short hair made the lice easier to deal with.

So I looked like a boy and I was in the boys' gang, and I thought? hoped? I'd grow up into a private eye.

And I did, as a sideline to my TV research job. But much of what I knew about the world and almost all my ethics were courtesy of those solitary, cynical, independent, brave men. I suppose they'd been my fathers. I didn't have a father myself. So in going to America, I was going home.

I'd thought Barty knew most of this and could have guessed the rest. We hadn't discussed it, but one of Barty's great attractions for me was that he knew more than he ever discussed, about everything. When I told him about my trip I expected to be told to enjoy myself and left alone to get on with it.

But instead what I got was a virulent outbreak of 'me-too'. 'I'm free – I'll come with you.' 'Let's stay at the Drake – I'll pay.' 'I'll show you Chicago; I know it well.' 'Let's fly First Class – give me your tickets, I'll trade them in and pay the difference.' 'We can spend some *quality time* together.'

Quality time? Had he been sneaking away to join New Man workshops?

I looked at him oddly, and I stalled.

Then it got worse. He tried to co-opt my friend Polly.

We were in London, of course. Polly was temporarily in Hong Kong: you'd have thought that was safe enough. But last Saturday morning when Barty and I were lounging about my place recovering from a good night in bed (ever noticed sex can be terrific when you're angry?) Polly rang, and Barty answered. He told her about the Chicago trip and (can you believe it? I couldn't) asked her to join us there.

Join us! As far as I was concerned, there wasn't going to *be* an us. There was going to be me and my dads and America.

Polly jumped at it. We're good friends, and close. She has the other flat in my building. But she'd been away for five months and in the last few weeks I'd had several pointless-chat calls from her. She was warming up to tell me something. She'd even suggested popping over to London for a weekend, but we hadn't been able to match dates.

When Barty handed her over to me, I was submerged in a Polly-torrent. 'That's wonderful – I'll book right after we get off the phone – I love Chicago, great shopping, and Frank Lloyd Wright, and, oh, Alex, I have missed you – we can catch up – I've so much to tell you – so much – I can't wait – where are we staying?'

'Wait a sec, Polly—'

'What hotel? I didn't get that—'

I took a deep breath. 'Polly, listen—Chicago isn't a

good idea. We won't have time to talk. Come over to London, OK?'

'But I keep trying, and you're never *free*!' she wailed.

'I will be. I promise.'

'When?' she demanded.

'Right after I get back from America. I'm free for a week.'

'Promise and swear? Cross your heart and hope to die? Girl Guides honour?'

'I wasn't a guide. Tanner's honour will have to do.'

'*Terrific!* I'll book now!'

When I got back to London, I'd hoped to have a week free to catch up with paperwork, sort out my tax records and receipts for the accountant, and spring-clean the flat. But she sounded delighted and determined and, in that mood, you can't stop Polly. Plus I'm fond of her, so I wouldn't have tried.

But when I rang off, I gave Barty the dirtiest of dirty looks, which he ignored. He was up to something: I didn't know what, and wasn't going to ask in case it opened up issues I didn't want to address.

'So it'll be just the two of us,' he said. 'You're probably right, it'll be more fun.'

'Quality fun,' I said, bitterly.

'Unless there's some special reason you want to be alone?'

I was beaten. My motives were too personal and perhaps too adolescent to air.

'No reason,' I said blandly, and stomped off to the bath.

We landed at Chicago at sixteen-thirty local time. It was raining, overcast, and chilly, colder than London had been, and the airport was almost as busy as Heathrow and better organized, newer-looking. We queued for Immigration in silence, neutral in Barty's case, hostile in mine. I didn't listen to his silence for long, though, because I loved the American voices straight from Central Casting.

The Immigration man was old and tired. He studied my passport in silence. Then he stamped it and handed it back to me with a huge white-toothed smile. 'Welcome to the United States!' he said. 'Enjoy!'

I smiled back. I'd try. And I'd be back. Alone.

Barty and I shared a taxi. At least we weren't staying at the same hotel. I'd refused to budge from the Black-stone, so I was staying there (wherever it was). I'd also insisted Barty stay someplace else, so he was booked at the Hilton.

After a silent taxi ride (I wasn't talking to Barty, he had more sense than to try to talk to me, and the taxi-driver couldn't speak English) through driving rain and grey, motorway/city landscapes which disappointingly reminded me of the outskirts of Paris, we stopped at a side door of a battered-looking, elegant building with a canopy and my hotel sign, and I got out. The driver started unloading both our bags. I tried to explain to him that Barty was going on, but Barty stopped me.

'I get off here,' he said.

'Not at my hotel,' I said, through gritted teeth. 'We agreed, I'll be working, I need space.'

He waved his arm at the towering newish bright building across the street. 'That's the Hilton,' he said.

We were in separate hotels, as I'd wanted. But the hotels were next door to each other.

Round two to Barty.

He paid the taxi.

I took the receipt. The amount was left blank, to make expense-fiddling easier, I supposed.

My kind of place, America.

I went, alone, up the narrow stairs to the Blackstone lobby. It was a big, shabby area, late-Victorian (what did they call Victorian in the US?) would-be impressive, scattered with high-backed chairs, some occupied, arranged around little tables. There was ornate metalwork on the lifts, a staircase off to a mezzanine floor, and elaborate glass-metalwork doors to a bar which advertised LIVE JAZZ! It was closed and dark. There'd be another bar somewhere, I hoped. And a coffee-shop where I could order two eggs over easy, like Lew Archer, or blueberry muffins like Spenser.

The reception desk was at the back. I checked in with a thirty-fiveish man, off-hand but competent, who didn't look at me once but scrutinized my credit card and passport. Then he gave me a key.

I took the key and clasped it. My room. My solitary room. It was past midnight British time and I was beginning to flag, but I knew a bath would revive me. I had to keep going for another five hours or so otherwise I'd wake up too early, local time. I'd got rid of Barty for the evening. I'd go for a long walk.

My room was terrific – on the sixth floor, big, with a television, two double beds, a window I could open, and a bathroom with a huge bath and a fixed shower. I turned both bathtaps on full, said 'Hi! Enjoy!' to the spider who scuttled up the tiled walls, went back into the bedroom and pulled my leather jacket off.

Then someone knocked on the door.

It had to be Barty. Or the hotel rapist.

'Who is it?' I called.

'Is that Alex Tanner, private investigator?' It was a female voice. British.

'Yes.'

'I'm a friend of Polly's. She said you'd help me.'

'To do what?'

'To find the love of my life.'

Chapter Two

I let her in.

I turned off the bath.

I came back into the room, and looked at her.

She was about my age (nearly thirty) and about six months pregnant. A very tall woman, not just tall compared to me (I'm short), and long-legged, with broad shoulders narrowing to slender hips. She was fair with longish hair plaited and knotted on top of her head, and a round, featureless, amiable, freckled face like a steamed sultana pudding. She was wearing grey leggings and Nikes under a floppy pink sweater, and no make-up or jewellery beyond the gold sleepers in her ears. She carried an expensive-looking cream cashmere coat and a weathered brown leather overnight bag.

I hoped she wasn't planning to overnight with me.

'Do sit down,' I said. I sat down at the writing desk at the far end of the room and pointed her to a chair beside it. 'What's this about Polly?'

'I was staying with her in Hong Kong last week and I told her about – about what had happened to me, and what I should do, and then she told me about you, and I knew I had to see you. It was wonderful because you were going to be here while I'm in Toronto – which is where I'm visiting friends this week – so I took a plane down this afternoon. I'm Jams Treliving.' She had a small, whispery voice, and a trick of fixing her eyes on yours and then, keeping the eye-contact, making little would-be appealing faces. A mannerism which she was twenty years too old for and at least a foot too tall.

'I didn't catch your first name,' I said.

'It's a nickname. I spell it J-a-m-s.'

She was still standing. I pointed to the chair again. She smiled and sat.

Silence.

Her sweater looked designer hand-knit, with a complicated pattern of gambolling lambs and puffy clouds and a meadow dotted with flowers. 'When are you going back?' I said.

'Tonight. When we're finished here. I didn't know how long it would take . . . I've never met a female private detective before.'

'What do you do?'

'I'm a model. I'm taking time out now till I have the baby, of course.'

Silence again. I'd never met a model with a face like a steamed pudding before, but I could hardly say that. Was she fantasizing?

'And you want to hire me to find the love of your life?'

She nodded and smiled. 'D'you mind if I smoke? I know I shouldn't, but since I knew I was pregnant I've allowed myself one a day. I didn't think one would count. I usually smoke forty.'

'Fine by me,' I said, and passed her an ashtray. It was the first time I'd warmed to her; up to then she'd seemed a wannabee-winsome little girl in a strapping Stepford Single body, too innocent for even minor vices.

She lit up, crossed her legs, and swung the top foot.

I opened my organizer. 'Give me some details.'

She looked puzzled.

I lost patience. 'Am I looking for a man? A woman? A dog?'

'A man,' she said. 'The father of my child.' She smiled pleadingly, hugged herself with her arms, and twined her long legs around each other. 'Go easy on me,' her body language said, 'I'm sensitive.'

I took a deep breath and reminded myself that when I'm tired I have the patience and people-skills of a buzz-saw, and that some people who projected 'I'm sensitive' actually were, and that she'd taken the trouble to get on a plane to see me.

'Where did he go missing?' I said.

'Here,' she said. 'In Chicago.'

'That's going to be difficult. I'm only here for three days, I've got an assignment already, and I have no contacts. You need a local detective. If you want, I'll hire one for you.' I'd enjoy that. A real private detective, with a gold shield left over from his time in the police, and underworld contacts, and a huge gun, and a disastrous private life which I knew better than to involve myself in. Didn't I?

She smiled. 'I want you,' she said. 'I'll pay you at your full-time rate for every day you're here.'

That meant double pay because Alan was paying me a daily rate for the drugs research, of course. Usually I'd have jumped at it. Apart from everything else, it would cover the Delta five-flight ticket which I'd never get to use. But she was a friend of Polly's, so I tried to put her off again.

'Really, Jams, I won't be able to do much.'

'That's up to me,' she said. 'It's my money,' and she took a British chequebook from her overnight bag. 'I'll pay you in advance, in pounds. Three days. What's your rate?'

I told her and she made out the cheque. 'What about expenses?' she said.

'I'll invoice you later. Who am I looking for?'

'An Englishman at the University of Chicago.' She fished around in her bag and passed me a brown envelope. 'There's all you'll need in there: my address and telephone number in London, and his name and last known address, with some personal details and a photograph.'

I took the envelope. 'Why are you carrying this about with you?'

'I've been thinking about hiring a detective for a while. But I couldn't . . . I didn't really want to find out.'

'Why not?'

'Because until I know what happened, I can make

it up. I can avoid it. I can dream. Never mind . . . What else do you need to know?

'Is he a professor at the University?'

'Oh no. A graduate student.'

'And you just want me to find him?'

'That's right.'

'Does it matter if he knows I'm looking for him?'

'Not at all.'

'And if I find him, what do I do?'

'Send him all my love. But you won't find him.'

'Why not?'

'Because he's dead. Or dreadfully injured, or in a coma.'

She spoke with such utter certainty that I was taken aback. Most missing person cases were simple, though, and the facts of this one seemed no different. An Englishman in Chicago should leave a trail a mile wide – I supposed, knowing nothing of Chicago. 'How long has he been missing?'

She stubbed out her cigarette, lit another one. 'I don't know.' She saw my raised eyebrows. 'I don't know exactly. I know where he was last September. September twenty-first.'

'And where was that?'

'On a British Airways flight, with me. From Heathrow to O'Hare. I last saw him by the luggage carousel. My bags came through first, he was still waiting for his, so I took mine and went. I didn't' – she blinked, and though there were no tears there was the echo of them – 'I hate long goodbyes, don't you?'

I did. And I didn't want to chat; I wanted her out

16

and myself in a bath. I usually like to get the feel of a client and of the situation I'll be mixing in to, but I was beginning to feel sandbag-tired. Still, I was taking her money.

'Yes,' I said. 'Especially with lovers.' I nodded at the high-riding bulge under her sweater. 'And you were lovers, obviously.'

'Oh, yes,' she said. 'Yes. We are. We still will be, after death. We'd talked about marriage. I told you, he's the love of my life. And I am of his.'

She was only pushing thirty. How would she know? How can you name, until your deathbed, the love of your life? But she evidently meant it literally, and she was crying now, frankly. I passed her a hand-ful of missing-man-size paper tissues.

'I'm sorry, Jams. Why are you so sure something's happened to him?'

'Because otherwise he'd have written. Or rung. I didn't expect to hear from him until I got back to London a week later – I was on a shoot in the back-woods up by the Lakes, and I hadn't a telephone number to give him, and he didn't have a telephone in his room – but then I waited, but the letter didn't come, and the post takes a while from America but I thought he'd write straight away and so it could even have been waiting for me when I got back but it wasn't, but he might have been coming back to England so I waited another week and then I called the place he was staying at in Chicago, and left a message, but he didn't return it, so I left another, and then I wrote, and then I wrote again, and then I wrote again . . .'

I gave her another wodge of tissues. 'And he didn't write back,' I said. 'Why don't you stay over in Chicago and look for him yourself?'

'I don't want to hear it myself, whatever it is. I want someone else to hear it for me, and then tell me, and soften it somehow. Because it means so much. Don't you see?' She was still crying, gently, the kind of tears that come from a long, deep hurt. The man had probably dumped her: it would turn out to be as simple as that. But it wasn't so simple for her, or it was simple but it was almost unendurable. Either way, now I had stirred it up, I couldn't just leave it and push her out on to the Chicago streets with her wound freshly opened.

I took a deep breath. 'Tell me all about it,' I said. 'How you met, how long you've known him, how much you saw each other, how often he wrote, what your plans were, what he was like – the whole bit. Give me the picture.'

It took her a moment to understand what I said. Then understanding clicked in her eyes, and she nodded eagerly. 'Yes, please. The more you know the better chance you have of finding him, isn't that true?'

'Probably,' I said.

She took a deep breath. 'I'll tell you everything,' she said. 'Anything you want to know, just ask.' She blew her nose with inelegant, childlike thoroughness, wadded the tissues, looked for a waste-paper basket and then, not finding it, shoved the tissues into her bag.

'Right,' I said. 'Let's start at the beginning. When did you meet him?'

'Twenty-first September last year,' she said.

I wrote it down. Then I looked at it. 'But that's when you last saw him,' I said.

She nodded. 'That's right.'

'So when you lost touch with him – when he went missing, you think – you'd actually *known* him for how long?'

'Ten hours,' she said.

Chapter Three

You don't find the love of your life on a flight from Heathrow to O'Hare. You might meet him but his importance wouldn't emerge till later. Would it?

Plus she claimed to be a model and I wasn't convinced.

I looked at my watch. Seven-fifteen, local time. One-fifteen tomorrow morning, London time. Hong Kong was eight hours ahead, so nine-fifteen Monday morning Polly-time. She'd be at her office, crunching numbers and calculating her bonus.

Jams gazed at me.

'I could murder a cup of coffee,' I said.

'I'll ring room service,' she said helpfully.

I don't use room service. Even on expenses. It takes for ever, the mark-up's outrageous and I never know how much to tip. Even if I ever did, I certainly wouldn't now. 'There must be a coffee-shop downstairs. Be a love and get us some take-out while I shower, then we can talk. Two coffees, white, no sugar, and a doughnut for me.'

'OK,' she said obligingly. 'Any special kind of doughnut?'

'The round kind.'

'OK.'

As soon as the door closed behind her I was by the phone wrestling with the international dialling instructions. Click click click click click silence buzz ring ring.

'Hello?'

'Hi, Polly.'

Silence, then recognition. 'It's you, Alex. Hi! I was expecting Tokyo!'

'Tokyo can wait. I'm at my hotel in Chicago and I've just met your batty friend Jams Treliving.'

'She's not batty. She's sweet, and she'll be a wonderful mother, it's so sad . . . when she told me she wanted a detective to find her man I knew it was fate sending her to you.'

'Why didn't you tell me she was on her way?'

'Because I thought you might put her off and I didn't want you to, and I knew if you saw her you'd agree to help her because you're a big softy.'

I didn't even bother to dispute this reading of my character, which struck me as risibly inaccurate, but pressed on for facts. 'Is she a model?'

'Of course, didn't she tell you?'

'But she's got a face like a pie.'

Polly laughed. 'Nobody uses her *face*, Alex. She's a leg model. That's why she's called Jams, you know, from the French, *jambes*. And a backside model. She was my bum in the health-food telly campaign back in the eighties, remember? When I ran laughing through the rain forest on to the beach, with the branches clawing at my face?'

'I remember.'

'The rear-view close-ups as I ran across the beach – that was Jams. My bum's too bony and flat. Hers is narrow and bippy.'

'Bippy?'

'You know, high and curved, so if you outlined her back with your hand, the buttocks stick out, bip. Very unusual in a white woman. And her front is good, too. Dead sexy without being obscene. She does knickers and stockings. She's the Sheer Heaven tights model – on all the posters and telly ads.'

'So she's successful?'

'Very. One of the three top in the world, I'd say.'

'What's she like?'

'I've told you, she's nice.'

'Polly, you think everyone's nice.'

'No, really, she *is* – she's down to earth, sensible, kind, very sensitive. One less protective skin than the rest of us and knits lovely sweaters. Everyone likes her.'

'What's her sex-life like?'

'Hasn't she told you, she's in love?'

'I know, since last September. I mean before that. Usually. Can she be sure who's the child's father?'

'Absolutely. She had a disastrous love affair which broke up about three years ago, and she hasn't slept with anyone since. She was waiting for the right man, she told me. That's what's so sad. She finds him and

22

then he vanishes. Make sure you find him for her. And give her my love.'

'Sure. Listen, Polly, should I expect any more of your lame dogs to turn up tonight? Because I was hoping to sleep.'

'Of course not, and Jams isn't a lame dog, and stop pretending you don't like clients, because you do. See you very soon.'

'See you soon.'

When I replaced the receiver I pulled a change of clothes from my suitcase and retreated into the bathroom.

Then I lay in the bath and thought about love.

I'd thought about it a great deal, recently.

Barty's about fifteen years older than me, he's been married before, he's got no children. And I was beginning to suspect he wanted to marry me and father some.

Marriage. Children. Serious stuff that I had to think through.

My childhood dreams hadn't included marriage. They'd been fantasies about independence – financial and emotional. Although I had, briefly, dreamed of being married to Lew Archer, Ross Macdonald's private eye. He's battered and middle-aged and world weary, and when I was about thirteen I thought I could bring the light of hope back into his bleak, knowing eyes. Then as I grew older and got to know more about boys I'd thought I'd stick to trying to get the light of hope back into my own, trying to get myself established, trying to get away from the Social Services, trying to be just me.

Now, I didn't know. I didn't know if the desire for independence was truly adult or just adolescent. I didn't know if my life would be hopelessly crippled, even if I didn't see it, by being Alex Tanner, woman detective and television researcher. People get crippled by the narrowness of their dreams, and my dreams had narrowed to a small tunnel.

OK, I was independent. OK, I earned enough money; plenty of research work came my way. OK, the mortgage on my flat was beginning to come down and I was going to go into my thirties reasonably well provided for. But emotionally, I was beginning to feel the pinch.

I'd thought an affair with Barty would suit me, and up to a point it did. I liked his company, mostly, and I enjoyed him in bed. Leaving out early one-night stands, I'd never slept with anybody who I didn't quite enjoy in bed, which suggested to me that what I enjoyed was bed. But I'd started feeling something I hadn't before: my body was tugging at me for babies.

I've never liked babies, much. I've never particularly liked puppies either, or kittens, and I never had fluffy toys, and when I was a small kid and crying into my pillow because my mother had gone off her head again I didn't hug a stuffed toy. I cried myself out and then I read a book, because books were the escape into other worlds, better than the one I was in. When I grew up, I'd be in those other worlds.

But now the other worlds seemed to me tawdry.

And narrow. After you've swaggered about the streets saying to yourself 'myself alone' for a while, that isn't enough. I half-wanted to be a full member of the human race, and I wasn't sure how I was going to do it, or even what it meant.

How did you become a full member of the human race? You took part, that was how. You gave parts of yourself away and other people or other groups gave parts of themselves back, and you were knitted together, and you went ahead like that, carrying other people and them carrying you.

But marriage. And children. Words that cast a long shadow, if you weren't sure, if you weren't in love. And I didn't think I was in love with Barty, but I didn't know. If I was, why did I grind my teeth with rage when he left his used teabags on my clean work-surfaces? Why did I think his back was too bony? Why did I still flirt with tasty men at wrap parties?

I didn't even know if there was such a thing as love. Not the thunder-and-lightning love, where your eyes met, and you knew, and it lasted for ever. Perhaps that only happened in Hollywood and Harlequin novels.

But Jams thought it had happened to her, and she was back with the coffee, I could hear her moving about in the bedroom.

I had to listen anyway. And who knows? I might learn.

Monday, 28 March

Chapter Four

I woke up before dawn, just after five.

In America.

Jams had left to catch her return flight before ten, and I'd crashed out and slept for seven hours: long enough to recover from the flight. Almost long enough to look forward to meeting Barty for breakfast.

To keep sulking this morning would be rude. I try not to be rude. It betrays too much.

And besides, it's rude.

I showered, using the free hotel-gel. I'd save the British Airways stuff for later. I unpacked and hung up my clothes, more than I would have brought if I'd been alone. I put on my newest jeans, my most expensive sweatshirt (black, no logo), and moussed my hair. It's still short. Not quite cropped, but short. And I dye it red. My natural hair is mouse but I don't feel mouse, I feel red.

There was no coffee-making equipment in the room. I couldn't do anything without coffee, so I fetched myself some, roaming the deserted hotel in search of a machine. The coffee-shop didn't open until six, I noticed: it was shuttered and dark. But there was a blessed machine on the ground floor near the reception desk with its sleepy young female receptionist. I got myself three plastic cups of coffee and wrestled them up again in the lift, pressing the buttons with my elbow.

I drank the first cup looking out of the window into the early-morning darkness. There were some cars, some people, enough light to see that across the road there was a park. I sorted through the maps I'd got and picked out the tourist map. I always start with those: from small to large. The tourist map first, to get familiar with what the locals thought a visitor would like to know about their city. When I'd got that fixed in my mind, I'd move on to the bigger map, and then the bigger, so when I hired a car and drove around I knew roughly where I was.

The thing that struck me about Chicago – my first American city – was the blessed simplicity of it. Rome, Paris, Amsterdam, Munich, Strasbourg, Edinburgh, Birmingham, all cities I'd got to know, were higgledy-piggledy organic growths, but the American city-from-scratch grid system made everything easy.

I knew it from the books, of course, but here it grew before my eyes as I glanced from the scaffolding on the map in my hands to the gradually lightening streets outside.

The central part of the city, the part covered by my tourist map, was a north/south strip on the west coast of Lake Michigan. The hotel was on South Michigan Avenue, facing east. The park was Grant Park. Across the park was the lake. To the north, along

Michigan Avenue and across the Chicago River, was the smart shopping area. Polly'd know all about that. Lucky she wasn't with us.

More important to me was the car rental office, which I located three blocks north of the hotel. Walking distance, good. I was due there at nine. I didn't actually *need* a car, the police press relations people had said they'd drive me anywhere I wanted to go, but if I didn't rent a car Barty would and then he'd be giving me rides, which wasn't the point of the trip at all. Besides, there's nothing like driving in a place to get to know it, and I could bill it to Jams – Alan probably wouldn't have worn it. He's a cheapskate and he's known me too long.

At noon the police were picking me up. Before that, I could get started on Jams's missing man.

I emptied her information envelope and found his last address. International House, East 59th St. Fifty-ninth St wasn't on the tourist map – too far south – so I moved to a larger map. Not far at all, maybe six miles. Straight down Lake Shore Drive. It looked easy. I'd soon find out if it was, directly I picked up my car.

It was still only six o'clock and Barty wasn't due for breakfast till seven-thirty, so I settled down to my notes of the previous night's interview with Jams.

Her lover was called Jacob Stone and he was very tall, six-foot three, important I supposed for Jams who would have been that height herself in heels. He was twenty-six (bit young for her?) and a second-year graduate student in the English Department, working for his Ph.D. in eighteenth-century English Literature. He'd been an undergraduate at Christ Church Oxford, taken his degree when he was just twenty, then gone into a merchant bank until he'd saved enough money to pay for graduate school. He'd hated the bank, according to Jams. Everyone was obsessed with money. That seemed fair enough to me, and a peculiar objection for him to make. If he wanted to be among unmaterialistic people with a social conscience, he could have worked for the Liberal Democrats.

I read on and thought. If he was researching English Literature, particularly long-ago stuff, why was he in America? Maybe the University of Chicago had bought all our eighteenth-century materials. I didn't know enough about it to judge, and at any rate, at this stage, it didn't matter. I didn't have to understand him. I just had to find him.

Because I'd known I was tired, last night, I hadn't taken any chances on my judgement of what was relevant. I'd taped our conversation, of course, and also made notes of almost everything she said, and most of it was about love, as dull as you'd expect, second-hand. Their eyes had met. Their hands had met. Their minds had met. Then their bodies had met, in the rest-room (her word), and then they'd known, and they'd gone back to their seats and exchanged photographs and talked about their childhoods and past lovers and dreams for the future and whether Jams should wear white at their wedding.

Then they went back to the rest-room.

Then they talked some more.

Then they went back to the rest-room.

By now I'd have thought the white wedding question was pretty well settled (as far as I was concerned, she'd be lucky to get away with cream) but they'd decided on white because she was a spiritual virgin until they'd met – in her heart she'd always been waiting for him.

I flicked through the pages of blether looking for some facts. He came from the north of England, near Doncaster, from an ordinary home.

That's what she'd said, 'an ordinary home'. Her words, or his? Foreign to my ear: American English. Probably his, then, as he'd chosen the US for his future, and had presumably started the process of going native. What could he have meant by it? I thought Americans used it as a euphemism for 'working-class' or 'uneducated'. He probably meant 'not posh'. That's what I'd have meant, if I'd said it, not that I would because I've never come across an ordinary home. All homes are weird. It sounded evasive or defensive or outright untrue.

I wasn't going to waste time on it now, but I found a new page in my organizer, headed it *Jacob queries*, and wrote *?Chicago for 18c Eng Lit* and *?ordinary home*.

Back to my interview with the lovebird.

He was an only child. They were going to call their first child Jacob, if he was a boy, Jacob Stone Jr because by then Jacob Senior would have a teaching job at an American university and they'd make their home in America.

Would they? A small alarm bell rang in my head. Surely he'd find it hard to get a work permit? The US was getting tighter and tighter on immigration. I added ?*work permit* to my list.

Back to the interview again. By now we were on the kind of house they'd live in, but that depended on where he got his job. His choice was New England because he liked snow. In which case they would have a clapboard house. (What was clapboard?) Her choice was Seattle, Washington, in which case they'd have a ranch-style house, because of the weather, preferably overlooking the ocean.

At that point, tired of dreams, I'd asked Jams if, when she found she was pregnant, she'd considered abortion. She said she hadn't. Abortion was wrong. The baby was a sacred trust. Any baby was, but particularly Jacob's.

I kept flicking through my notes. Ah. His father had died when Jacob was twelve. His mother had died recently – he was returning from her funeral. He'd been deeply upset by his mother's death, Jams said, because he was such a sensitive caring man.

I sighed. Everyone was upset when their mother died. Still, she was biased. And I was biased too, because I disliked the word 'caring'. It was usually used to describe the kind of person who asked you how you were in a sincere voice and didn't listen to the answer, who would give you only what they wanted you to have and who would be out of the door like a rabbit if you actually asked them for anything difficult. And the people who used it behaved like that themselves.

I looked at the photograph of Jacob that he'd given her and that she had, reluctantly, given me. It was a graduation photograph, therefore presumably five years old. It showed two people standing in bright sunlight in an ornately carved stone doorway. Jacob wore a dark suit mostly covered by a gown. He was goodlooking in an anonymous way, with smallish features and plenty of dark curly hair under his mortarboard. He was looking straight ahead, his shoulders squared either tensely or in an attempt to look assertive and masculine. The woman beside him, surely his mother, was gazing devotedly up into his face. She was old and plain and seemed not to care. Her thinnish grey hair was centre-parted and plaited unflatteringly close to her lumpy head. She was wearing a black blouse buttoned right up to the neck and at her wrists, a long shapeless black skirt and low-heeled black leather shoes. She had puffy ankles and hands. Her loving smile showed long yellow teeth in a nearly lipless mouth.

I knew little about him from the photograph, but more about her. I certainly wouldn't have wanted to come between them. If he was the love of Jams' life, then she was lucky that she hadn't had to cope with that particular mother-in-law.

But you couldn't judge much from a photograph and I was wasting time, because one visit to International House might settle it. There he'd be, perhaps a bit embarrassed, and gobsmacked when he heard he was nearly a father, and there Jams would be with another disastrous end to the briefest of encounters. And there I'd be with three days' pay for one day's work.

I went through the rest of the notes and the only thing that struck me was that he'd said he was close to finding the truth about himself. That was embedded in a lot of detail about the things they'd told each other about themselves, and I'd made myself a promise from the start that I wouldn't sneer because they were speaking from the heart, and the more one speaks from the heart the sillier, usually, it sounds. Hearts aren't sophisticated. So I didn't sneer but I wondered what he meant when he said he was close to finding out the real him. It was in the loop.

I read my notes again. 'The real him was in the loop.'

Q: The loop?
A: Yes, that's what he said.
Q: What did he mean?
A: I asked him that. He said he'd tell me when he knew, he was just working it out.

The loop. It meant nothing to me. Except that I'd just seen it written on the map. The Loop was an area of central Chicago. Had he been referring to that?

I added it to my list of queries. *? The loop*.

Then Barty knocked on the door. Time for breakfast.

Chapter Five

Just after nine I was heading south on Lake Shore Drive in my hired Mazda listening to a local country and western station. The weather was forty degrees and clear, as the radio told me repeatedly in between the old-style country songs where victim women bewailed the loss of their men, and new-style country songs where women stood up to their men, kept their self-respect, but lost the men anyway.

Losing a man wasn't my present problem. In the short time I'd been in America so far, I'd noticed my pulling-power was appreciably increased, almost as if a huge banner reading 'tasty piece' hovered over my head and marked me out from the crowd. The waiter in the coffee-shop, men in the street, and the man in the car-hire office had all looked at me and looked again, interested.

It was the glut syndrome. I've noticed it before. Take one job and you're offered others: make one friend and more line up: involve yourself in a love affair and other men start sniffing the air. During the last few months with Barty, it had been happening in England, but it was flowering here.

I stopped for a traffic light, glanced at the driver next to me, and looked away when he smiled. The sky was blue, the clouds were small and puffy, and I was being paid double time. Hallelujah!

Breakfast had gone well. I'd tried to mend fences: Barty'd responded with his usual deftness, managing to convey simultaneously 1) no fences had been shattered 2) he accepted the apology I wasn't giving 3) he'd keep out of my hair for the rest of the day. We'd eat about eight.

Once we'd got that sorted, I'd felt warm enough towards him to tell him about Jams and Jacob. By this time I was on my second cup of coffee – the States has a brilliant system where the waiter keeps topping you up. You don't even have to catch his eye and you're not charged extra. Funny, really, since the Americans I'd met in England seemed to regard caffeine as a threat to health second only to cigarettes, and way, way more dangerous than cocaine. Perhaps I moved in the wrong circles.

'So you're moonlighting,' Barty'd said.

'Yes.'

'Take care.'

In pursuit of Jacob I wasn't taking care. There was no care to take. There was just fun work to look forward to, and a new place, and my whole life. 'Yes!' I said, out loud, and nearly missed the exit for Hyde Park, the University of Chicago area.

The University itself was in a very broad tree-lined and grassy avenue, a series of stone buildings, massive, aiming at Gothic. Pity it hadn't totally missed. Not handsome, but monolithic. There was nowhere legal to park near International House so I pulled on to a grass verge and went in.

It was like a barracks. Tall ceilings, echoing floors, walls painted in neutral khaki-ish tones. I wasn't sure I'd have chosen to live there. Perhaps for a term while I got myself sorted out in a foreign country. But for a year? Maybe Jacob didn't notice where he lived.

The woman at the reception desk was of Asian origin, I thought, then lurched into political correctness panic, as if she could read my mind. Asian-American, that sounded better; I readjusted my internal comment. The woman was Asian-American, about my age, dressed in jeans and several layers of thin wool sweaters in shades of mustard. She had short black hair and thick glasses and she was reading an electronics textbook with fierce concentration. When I spoke, it took her a moment or two to focus on me, but then she answered readily enough after consulting her computer. No, Jacob Stone was not in residence. Yes, he had been. He'd moved out. Last September. Yes, he'd left a forwarding address which she scribbled down for me.

I looked at it.

> **c/o Nabokov,**
> **Apartment # 1,**
> **49 Humbert St,**
> **Chicago**

Graduate student humour. Very funny. The hairs lifted on the back of my neck. If this was a genuine forwarding address, I was Oprah Winfrey. Jacob Stone had just done a vanishing act, and I had an interesting case. I hoped.

'That'll be off Lolita Avenue, I suppose,' I said.

'Excuse me?' The receptionist looked puzzled. Not a novel-reader, and why should she be? If she'd made a reference to electronics I wouldn't have picked it up.

'Sorry, just talking to myself. Is there really a Humbert Street? Have you ever heard of it?'

'Sure. Two blocks north. Off Kenwood.'

I produced the map, she showed me, and I walked there, checking on the hire car as I passed. No parking ticket yet, though I didn't care if I got one. They wouldn't extradite me for parking.

Humbert Street was a narrow side-street of small-ish detached wooden houses surrounded by scrubby grass. The houses were half-familiar to me from films. They weren't decaying but they weren't being scrupulously maintained either, and by each front door was a cluster of bells. Multiple occupation, student lets.

Number 49. In better condition than most, painted pale grey, the windows and front door white. I went up the steps to the raised verandah and across it to the door, and looked at the names on the bells, not expecting to find Nabokov.

But there it was. *C. Nabokov.* I'd jumped to con-clusions and been wrong. Come to think of it, with two hundred plus million people of assorted ancestry and God knows how many streets which they'd had to name from scratch, I'd probably also find an Austen on Mansfield Park, a Dostoevsky in Karamazov Avenue, a Beethoven on Emperor Street and a Death living on Salesman.

I rang the bell, and I could hear it buzzing in the room by the front door, on the right. Apartment Number 1 for sure.

No answer. I peered in at the window – large room, assorted rental furniture including a desk and the kind of sofa that collapsed into an uncomfortable bed, piles of books and papers, computer, sound system, scattered CDs. Graduate student.

I couldn't make out the titles of the books so I didn't know whether they were likely to be Stone's. His name wasn't on the bell but he mightn't have bothered to put it there – anyone likely to call would probably know that he was living with C. Nabokov. I wondered whether C. Nabokov was female, in which case I'd have bad news for Jams.

I rang the bell again and then pressed all the others, on spec. An upstairs window opened and an expressive-faced tousled young Mexican looked out. (Hispanic? Mexican-American? Puerto Rican? Never mind, my thoughts were my own.) He started by look-ing annoyed, then gave me a 'Hi-there!' smile.

I smiled back. He smiled more widely. So did I. Then I reckoned I'd better speak before the dental escalation cracked our jaws. Besides, his teeth were whiter than mine and he seemed to have more of them.

'I'm looking for C. Nabokov,' I said.

'Apartment One.'

'I've tried. There's no answer.'

'Then Carl's out.'

Carl. Usually a man's name. But John Wayne had started life as Marion. 'Is Carl a woman?'

'Not that I've noticed. But we're not real close.' He laughed. I laughed.

'I'm actually looking for someone who was staying with Carl, Jacob Stone. Do you know him?'

'Sure. He's British, like you.'

'Is he staying here now?'

'I haven't seen him around for a while. D'you want to come up?'

'No thanks. Not right now. When do you think Carl will be back?'

'He's in most evenings.'

'OK. Thanks again. I'm Alex Tanner, by the way.'

'Glad to know you, Alex. I'm Raul. Raul Escobedo.' He gave me a final smile and wave and closed the window behind him. I took one of my *Alex Tanner Private Investigator* cards and scribbled a note to Carl Nabokov, giving him the number of my hotel and asking him to ring me.

Then I went back to the car. I needed to be back at the Blackstone to be picked up by the police by noon, and I couldn't be late for that. Plus, to be fair to Alan, I had to run over the drugs doco notes one last time. Just because the job he'd given me was easy didn't mean I couldn't make a mess of it. In fact I was more likely to, because I'd have to force myself to concentrate. So I drove back to the hotel to meet the police and do the work that Alan Protheroe was paying me for.

'Oh, God,' said Barty. It was a long, exhausted, grateful moan. I pushed lightly and he rolled away from me and lay on his back, arms flopping outwards. 'Where's my pillow?' he said.

'On the floor at the end of the bed, I think. Why don't you look?'

'Look for me, woman.'

'In your dreams.'

I didn't move. He fetched the pillow and settled himself comfortably.

'That was terrific,' I said. It had been. I wondered why. Maybe I was feeling more attractive. Maybe I was trusting Barty more.

Whatever it was, I liked it. I punched my own pillows more comfortably under my head and settled back, close to Barty, my side pressed to his side all the way down, though because he was so much taller his side went on longer. The hair on his leg was rough. I rubbed my leg against it, felt the drying sweat, felt almost part of him.

'What's the time?' he said.

'I squinted at my clock. 'Five past nine.'

'We've missed our table.'

'Where were we going?'

'Never mind, you're not interested.'

'True,' I said. I wasn't. Barty liked poncy restaurants. He said he liked good food and most good food was only to be found in poncy restaurants. That could have been true. I didn't think any food was worth the price he so often paid. 'Are you hungry?' I asked.

'Not really . . . my stomach still thinks it's in London, and three in the morning. Are you?'

'Not enough to get up for.' I yawned and stretched and cuddled back into the crook of his arm.

'Don't worry, I'll leave you alone soon.'

'I'm not worried,' I said, a little surprised that he'd so misjudged my mood. I didn't want him out. I was only pleasantly tired. 'Ask me about my day,' I said.

'So, how'd the drugs research go?' he said.

'It's not research proper, just mopping up for Alan. It went fine. You know the American police better than I do. They're much more media-oriented than us. They were disappointed that I didn't want to make a major motion picture and cordon off the streets of central Chicago. I just need some exterior shots of a drug-ridden housing project and a war-zone high school, and then the talking head.'

'Who is it?'

'A policeman. Commander in the Third Division. A lovely man, good-looking and very clued up. So that's all finished.'

'And the missing person case?'

In a minute, I'd tell him. First: 'Barty, have you ever fallen in love at first sight?' I asked.

'Certainly,' he said promptly. 'When I was at school.'

'Who with?'

'I can't remember her name,' he said.

'What can you remember?'

'Her legs.'

'Jams has fantastic legs, of course,' I said, conscious of my rather stubby numbers. 'But do you believe in it? Love, like that?'

His head was higher than mine, and he bent forward to peer at my face. 'Is this a fish?' he said.

'Absolutely not. I was thinking about Jams, about whether it was possible, what she said.'

'The Sicilians call it "the thunderbolt",' he said.

'I've seen *The Godfather* too,' I said. 'And I don't care if the Maltese call it "the falcon". That isn't what I asked. Do you think it's possible? Really?'

'Yes, I do. All you need are the preconditions.'

'Which are?'

'Mutual lust and a seeking heart,' he said, stroking my hair.

'Who said that?'

'I just did.'

'It *sounds* good. Is it true?'

'I think so. That's why I fell in love with Miranda.'

His first wife. Of whom I was still, sometimes, a little jealous. I prodded round in my emotions for jealousy and didn't find any. 'And then what happened?'

'I married her. And I loved her. And then it went away.'

'Went away?'

'Gone, vanished, departed. I don't know if it happened suddenly, but I knew it suddenly. One day I just looked at her and I didn't love her.'

'So then what did you do?' I asked, rather uncomfortably. Maybe one day he would look at me, too, and not love me.

'I tried to make the marriage work.'

'But it didn't?'

'No.'

'Why?'

'Because Miranda didn't want it to. She wanted me to love her. Not just day-to-day love, but thunderbolt love.'

'Did she love you like that?'

'No. She never had.'

Too many cans of worms, I thought. Not now, I decided, and made an effort not to pull away from him. He patted me on the shoulder and re-settled himself, further away from me.

'What you're saying then is that you believe it happens, but it doesn't last?'

'I don't see how it can. It's infatuation more than love.'

'So maybe I won't be doing Jams a favour even if I find Jacob for her.'

'But you'll try to, anyway. Do I gather that he's really gone missing?'

I told him what I'd done that morning.

'And the Carl Nabokov chap hasn't called back?' he said when I'd finished.

'Not yet. I'll try him again tomorrow. If I go over early, maybe he'll still be in. Unless students here keep different hours to English ones.'

Tuesday, 29 March

Chapter Six

Next morning, I woke at four-thirty, still partly running on London time, and spent an hour finishing my notes for Alan and sorting the location Polaroids. Then I went back to sleep again.

When the telephone rang at nine, it startled me. I didn't recognize the ring. A single ring, like continental Europe. I fumbled it to my ear. 'Hello?'

'Alex Tanner?'

'Yes.'

'Carl Nabokov here. I got your note. Too late to call last night. What can I do for you?'

'Wait a moment. I need to wake up.'

He gave a short, polite, 'get on with it' laugh.

'It's about Jacob Stone,' I told him.

'So your note said.' His voice sounded tense and I wondered why. Impatience? Shyness? Guilt?

'I'm looking for him. Do you know where he is?'

'Sorry, no. I haven't seen him since he went back to England last fall.'

'When was that?' I'd got my notebook now, and found the page.

'Last September sometime. Right after he came

51

back to the States after his mother's funeral. When he moved out of International House.'

I scribbled. *Jacob > Chicago 21st Sept, with Jams. Jacob > London, soon after.*

On the flight he'd told Jams he might be in England, soon: it made sense. So why hadn't he been in touch with her? 'Do you have an address for him in England?'

'A hotel. I was supposed to meet up with him – I was in England working at the British Library. But he didn't show, and the hotel didn't know where he was.'

'Annoying for you,' I said, because that was what he sounded. Retrospectively irritated. Not worried.

'I guess,' he said.

'Could we meet? And talk?'

He hesitated. 'I'm kind of busy. I'm leaving Chicago Thursday.'

Thursday. The day after tomorrow. He could spare me a few minutes, at least, so I could see him face to face – when I'd woken up enough to sort out my questions.

I left my request in the silence, and waited.

He cleared his throat. 'What's your interest in Jacob, exactly?'

'You saw my card. I'm a private investigator. I've been hired to find him.'

'I've told you all I know. I don't see how I can help you.'

'I'll fit in with you,' I said. 'Any time today. Just for fifteen minutes. I'd be very grateful . . . what about lunch?'

'Can't make lunch.'

'A drink, then. Or a cup of coffee . . . I'll meet you anywhere you say.'

I had him. There was no way he couldn't manage it.

'Six o'clock, then,' he said, not entirely ungraciously. 'My place?'

'Six o'clock, your place.'

I put the phone down, went to the bathroom and brushed my teeth while the bath was running. Then I lay in the British Airways-scented water watching my spider working away on the ceiling and I began to come to life.

Jacob was well on the way to being a real missing person. A London hotel as his last address, if Carl Nabokov was telling the truth, and why shouldn't he be?

If he was, why the quick turnaround back to England? And after Jacob had accomplished whatever it was, had he meant to return to America? Jams believed he was going to continue with his Ph.D. But he may not have told her the truth.

One way of checking that would be to find out what, if anything, he'd told the university. He must have a tutor, or something. He must be paying tuition fees – or have stopped. And, perhaps even more usefully, he must have given a British address when he originally signed up.

But I had no contacts in the University of Chicago

at all, and they'd probably be very tight on personal information.

Then I sat up with a splash of water that frightened the spider, who scuttled across the ceiling and away.

I had no contacts at the university, but I did have university contacts. In England. And the academic world was both international and small.

It was early afternoon in England. I had hours of English telephone-time left.

A woman's voice answered on the second ring. 'Grace Macarthy.' Then she chuckled.

I'd only known Grace personally for a few days six months ago, when she was involved in one of my cases, but the chuckle brought her powerful, mischievous personality vividly into my hotel room, thousands of miles away as it was. I don't like Grace much, partly because she's an ex-lover of Barty's, partly because my part-time assistant Nick has a crush on her and dragged her name into every conversation until I told her to can it.

But when it comes to useful information, I never let feelings get in the way. Grace is an Oxford English don, an efficient Ms Fixit, and very conceited. I didn't think she could resist a challenge.

'Grace, this is Alex Tanner. We met last year, remember?'

'Of course I remember,' she said. 'Don't be silly.

As if Nick would let me forget. How are you? How's Barty?'

My spirits lifted. It sounded as if Nick was making Grace suffer too. 'We're both fine. I'm calling from America.' In other words, long-distance, don't let's chat.

'Oh, where?' she said conversationally, on purpose to tease me, I thought.

'Chicago.'

'I've never been to Chicago,' she said. 'Frank Lloyd Wright?'

'And sky-scrapers, the heart of the Midwest, the Golden Mile, Al Capone, David Mamet, the 1968 Democratic Convention, voting the dead in Cook County, *ER, The Fugitive*, splitting the atom, the Windy City and a toddlin' town,' I said, hoping to shut her up.

'Relax,' she said, chuckling again. 'That's enough warm-up, you can move to the workout. I suppose you want something. What is it?'

'Information. Which I don't actually think you'll be able to get, and which I need very quickly. By midnight tonight, your time.'

'Bet you a fiver I can,' she said.

'Bet you a tenner you can't,' I said.

Now she was laughing. 'And my father's a policeman. OK, Alex, give me your questions.'

Barty wanted us to spend the rest of the day together. I wanted to spend the whole day alone, but I didn't want to tell him why. It would have been altogether too intimate to say, 'I want to think. About me, about you, about the rest of my life.' It was enough, for the moment, that he was my lover. I didn't want him inside my head too.

So we compromised. I'd have a two-hour lunch break from togetherness.

It wasn't outside weather. Overcast, chilly, with lowering heavy clouds and rain carried on gusting winds from the lake. So in the morning we went to the Chicago Historical Society and talked about history.

We parted at noon. I'd been looking forward to it. But suddenly the two hours weighed heavy in my hands like obsolete coinage. I didn't want to think about life. For reasons which I knew I was not up to exploring, just living it was hard enough.

I went back to my hotel room. It was empty. What did I expect?

I wasn't hungry, but what do you do with a useless lunch break? You eat. You eat in the sort of place you eat by yourself, that you can go into wearing jeans and a sweat shirt and a leather jacket and Doc Marten boots. Not a Barty 'I've plenty of money or I've got a man who is and who'll spend it on me' sort of a place.

I walked north up Michigan Avenue. The lake wind was so cold I felt my scalp clamping round my skull. I walked three blocks and passed two universities. At least that's what they said they were, but as they offered vocational training and classes in lunch hours and after work, they looked more like colleges of further education to me.

If I'd been born in Chicago, would it have been different? Would I have got on, further, learning after work? Would I have survived at all? Amid these tall overwhelming inhuman skyscrapers, built for people with position and money, would I have shrivelled and died? Would my mother have lived in one of the bleak, violent housing projects the police had shown me, and would I have gone to a high school where the canteen only provided plastic cutlery to cut down on the stabbing deaths? Would I have been a stabber, or a stabbee?

Suddenly, powerfully, I was homesick.

I'd always assumed everywhere in the world was open to me. It was just a matter of getting there, on expenses. But if, abroad, I was going to whimper like a baby for Mum England, then that closed lots of doors.

I hate the sound of doors closing.

I needed something reassuring. One of my public homes.

So I went in to a Burger King.

I'd thought it would be familiar. Hamburger chains are the same all over the world. That's the point of them. Nobody'd go there for the food, not even me.

It wasn't familiar. It had a different system of ordering.

In England, you go up to the counter, and you order, and you pay, and you take it and perch yourself at a table on one of the chairs which are designed only to let you perch, because Burger King and McDonalds have worked out long ago what I was just beginning to click to, which is that the kind of loser who eats at a burger place has nowhere to go and will stay inside in the warm for as long as they can for the price of a cheap burger or even for the price of a cup of coffee – unless you provide chairs that put your back into spasm after ten minutes.

I thought I knew what to expect, though I didn't expect *not* to want it so powerfully. But when I reached the counter I gave my order and paid, but was then told to wait and pick up my order from a different assistant further along.

I didn't like it. But I did it, because I'd paid.

I waited for my number to be called. I took the bag. I perched myself on the familiar chair at the familiar table, and took out my food.

I'd ordered a cheeseburger and a large orange juice. I also had something else: an enormous flying-saucer of a hamburger, oozing mayonnaise. I investigated it. Tomato and onion-rings and burger and two cheese slices and pickle and, as I already knew, mayonnaise.

I looked at the receipt. There'd been a mistake. I had two receipts, printed out together. My order, which I'd paid for, taken by Antoinette. The oozing flying-saucer was a 'Whopper Cheese Com', and someone else had paid Latonya for it, and was presumably complaining at the counter as I read.

I ate my order. I packed up the Whopper Cheese Com in the bag and took it with me back to my room. It was disgusting, but it was free.

Then, with an hour to spare, I lay on the bed and waited for Barty.

I hate waiting. I try never to do it because so much of my childhood was wasted like that. Not waiting for something good to happen: waiting for anything to happen, all of it in someone else's control. But now I had none of my usual props. I couldn't clean my flat or file or type or get out there and hustle. I couldn't even read, because I hadn't brought any books. The television – all ten channels – was so dire I'd given up on it the day before.

When I heard Barty's knock on the door, I wasn't relieved, I was angry. With myself for being such an empty person, and with him for showing me.

He breezed in, pleased to see me. He went straight up to the Burger King bag on the dressing-table, looked inside, said 'It's freezing cold. What is it, the carryout hamburger Captain Oates went to fetch?'

I took a deep breath. It wasn't his fault, none of it was. It was partly circumstances and partly mine, and since circumstances weren't likely to surge forward and shoulder the burden of responsibility, that left me.

'I'm glad to see you,' I said.

Then we went to the Frank Lloyd Wright house and talked about architecture, and I began to feel better. Better enough for Barty to get on my nerves, again. He knew more about architecture than I did, as he had about Chicago's history in the morning, and was so informative and unassuming with it that my fingers itched for complimentary slippers to stuff down his throat – or, better still, a complimentary sledge-hammer.

By five o'clock I'd had more than enough, and we parted for the night. I'd said I was tired and that after my meeting with Carl Nabokov I'd go back to my hotel, eat Captain Oates's hamburger, and go to bed. Barty wasn't pleased but he knew better than to make it obvious, and we arranged to meet for breakfast the next morning.

Back in my hotel room the red light on the telephone was flashing. A message. I rang the desk. 'Grace Macarthy called,' they said.

Good. I dialled. Ring ring ring. 'Grace Macarthy.'

'Alex here.'

'You owe me a tenner. Have you got a pencil?'

'Fire ahead.'

'I'll give you the Oxford stuff first, OK? Stone's home address – 5 Ormskirk Drive, Armthorpe, Doncaster, South Yorkshire. No telephone number. As an undergraduate he was brilliant but peculiar. Few friends. Went home every weekend. Very religious. Fundamentalist. Belonged to a Northern sect.'

'Hang on,' I said, still scribbling. 'Right. Thanks.'

'The Chicago stuff wasn't easy. Here's what I got: he's known as conscientious, a hard worker, well informed, well organized, not much of a mixer, a bit formal, rather arrogant. He paid the fees for the autumn term – they call it a quarter – last September, earlier than he could have got away with. He didn't

60

register for any course in the autumn term, though. He should have done that in late September. They've heard nothing of him since.'

'So he didn't arrange for leave of absence?'

'No. So either he meant to come back, or he meant to drop out. And if he meant to drop out, why did he pay the fees?'

Thanks, Grace, I can work it out for myself, I thought. 'How good is your Chicago information?' I said.

'Reliable. From a friend of a friend. Didn't I do well?'

'Very well,' I said grudgingly.

'But I always do,' she said. 'Why does it irritate you?'

'Because I think you're smug,' I said, goaded. Which she'd meant me to be.

She chuckled. 'So are you,' she said sweetly, and rang off.

Chapter Seven

I don't know what I'd expected Carl Nabokov to look like. His voice on the telephone was a pleasant light baritone, nothing special. It hadn't prepared me for the breathtaking man who answered the door on my first ring.

'Hi,' he said. 'You must be Alex. I'm Carl.'

I should have said Hi and offered my hand, but what I did was stand and gape like an idiot. He was about five-ten or five-eleven, slender but muscular, with very dark, straight hair, grey-green eyes and extraordinary, beautiful skin. It was obvious he was of mixed race, but it wasn't at all clear how many races had gone into the melting-pot. A little black in the dusky bloom, a little Slav in the arched nose and high cheek-bones, perhaps some native American in the narrow, tilted eyes.

He was dressed like many of the graduate students I'd seen – red and blue plaid flannel shirt, no tie, brown corduroy trousers, cheap tweed jacket, cheap not-leather shoes – but the clothes didn't matter. He was easily the most physically attractive man I'd ever met. He was even the most attractive

man I'd ever seen; better than the young Robert Mitchum, who he rather resembled and who was my
acme of fanciability to date.

'Hi,' I managed. I wasn't going to risk a handshake.

He was staring back at me, probably because he
thought I was half-witted.

'Sorry I'm early,' I said.

'That's fine. Come on in,' he said, and led me into
the front room of his apartment, which was ready for
me. No trace of the lived-in disorder I'd seen through
the window the previous day. Now the books were on
shelves, the CDs on racks, the papers in files stacked
neatly on his desk.

He offered me a Coke. I accepted, and he went
through a narrow corridor to a small, half-visible
kitchen area. I could see a sink, a drainer and an
old bulky fridge, which was humming to itself and
hiccuped loudly in protest when he opened its door.

I sat on an upright chair with my back to the
window, looked around the room, breathed evenly,
and waited. I could hear him opening cans and
decanting the drink into glasses.

He brought them back on a tray. 'Caffeine-free,
sugar-free,' he said reassuringly. Yuk. I smiled, took a
glass and sipped. He sat down on the sofa, put the tray
and his glass on a low coffee-table, and clasped his
hands on his knees.

Then I began to relax, because he was as nervous
as I was. He was sweating lightly, looking at me
intently and then looking away again when he met
my eyes.

Mutual lust at first sight, perhaps. This could be fun. I thought. 'Thanks for seeing me,' I said.

'Yeah,' he said, then he cleared his throat, and got ready to say something he expected would be unwelcome. 'The thing is, Alex, you've had a wasted journey out here. I've been thinking. Jacob's my friend. I don't see that I should talk about him to you. His life's his own business, right? Whatever he wants to do, I guess that's up to him.'

'Maybe you could tell me the names of some of his other friends who'd be prepared to help.'

'That wouldn't be so easy. He's not – he doesn't make friends quickly.'

'How come he did with you?'

'We were in the same seminar. We're working in the same field. We just – took to each other. I helped him out some.'

'How?'

'Socializing. Like that. He's not a great mixer.'

'Is there something wrong with him?'

'What do you mean?'

'Something that makes him not fit in? Is he an oddball?'

'He's unusual, sure. His upbringing, I guess. You know he's very religious? Partly that. He's a serious person. Very – clear. Very directed.' Then he remembered. 'But I'm not prepared to talk about it, all right?'

'Of course,' I said. 'I understand. But I'm working for someone who loves him, who's concerned about him, who thinks he's in some kind of trouble.'

'And who would that be?' he said.

'Jams Treliving,' I said.

He took a deep breath. Of relief? 'Jacob hasn't been in touch with her?' he said.

'You know who I mean?'

'Sure. The woman he met on the flight.'

'What did he tell you about her?'

'Alex, I'm not going to discuss it.' He smiled apologetically. It was a very charming smile: self-deprecating, conspiratorial. I smiled back.

'OK,' I said. 'But where do you think he is? Did he mean to give up his Ph.D. course? It'd be odd, surely. He's spent three years on it already and presumably he still intends to work in universities. So he needs to get the qualification, to get a job.'

'That's his decision.'

'Of course it is, if he made it. But he didn't sign off from the university, did he? And that sounds as if he meant to come back.'

'How do you know?' he said, sipping his Coke, looking me up and down with his heavy-lidded, young-Robert-Mitchum eyes. Or maybe young-Al-Pacino eyes. Tasty as hell, anyway. I recrossed my legs and wished they were longer, better, sexier, and involuntarily fiddled with my hair then stopped my fiddling fingers because that's the deadest giveaway of all. He mightn't have known that, of course, though he probably would because a man like him would have been around block after block, surely.

Concentrate, Alex. This is work. 'I've contacts in the university,' I said. 'I know he paid the tuition fees for the autumn quarter. Which suggests he expected to be back to attend the courses.'

He cleared his throat, gestured with his hands. He had great hands, long, narrow, brown and strong-looking. 'See here, Alex, do you understand my position? I'm in a dilemma. If something serious has happened to Jacob, and maybe I could help, then that's one thing. I'll give you the address of the hotel we were supposed to meet, no problem. But as to telling you anything else, anything that was told me in confidence as a friend, well that's another consideration altogether.'

'I understand,' I said, though even through my lust it struck me as garbage. How confidential was a decision to drop out of university? 'Did he ever talk to you about a loop?'

'A loop? Do you mean the Loop, downtown?'

'I don't know what I mean. He mentioned it to Jams and said it was important, but he didn't say what it was.'

Carl shook his head. 'Not that I recall.'

'But he did talk to you about his feelings? You were close friends?'

'Were?' he said. 'You think he's dead?'

'Jams does.'

'Why?'

'Because she believes they fell in love, and nothing but death or terrible accident would prevent him getting in touch with her. She's a romantic.'

'And you're not?'

'I didn't come here to talk about me.'

'I wish you had,' he said. 'How're you fixed for the rest of the evening?'

Much too sudden. Were the courting customs in America so different? Was I sending out the wrong signals? Was it just the new tasty quick-scoring Alex, was he a nutter, was he hiding something?

I smiled non-committally. I didn't want to close him out completely, but I didn't want to have to wrestle with him either. 'I'm over here with a friend,' I said. 'I'm meeting him later, but thanks anyway . . . Look, it does seem as if Jacob's disappeared. I'm not asking for any confidences. Just a clue about his plans.'

'I'm sorry, that was out of line,' he said, and he blushed. His skin looked even more beautiful and I warmed to him further. Not a smooth operator: possibly sincere.

'Not at all,' I said Englishly. It was a pleasure, after Barty, to be dealing with someone less sophisticated than I was. 'Come on, help me out about Jacob. Jams is really worried. Should she be?'

'I guess so. He planned on coming back for the autumn quarter. He left most of his stuff here with me.'

'Great,' I said briskly. 'Let's take a look.'

Half-an-hour later I'd sorted through the things Jacob had left, and apart from finding out that the top of his sartorial range was Marks and Spencer and the bottom the cheapest of cheap market gear, that he wore boxer shorts until the waist elastic went without staining them (were there panty-liners for men?), that he had tiny writing and took good clear notes, that he liked classical music, particularly Bach and choral works, and that his doctoral dissertation was based around an eighteenth century sect-founding ex-vicar called Thomas Tubmaster, I was no further.

There were no personal letters at all, no diary, no address book, no photographs: as far as I could see, no clues. I sat back on my heels and surveyed the material. One suitcase, full of clothes. Four boxes, two of books, two of papers and notes and filecards and floppy disks and CDs, one portable CD player, one empty holdall.

We were in Carl's bedroom. It was just about big enough for a double bed and an old wardrobe. When he took Jacob's things out from under the bed and down from the top of the wardrobe, there was no floor space at all. So he'd been lying on the bed and watching me as I searched.

I replaced the floppy disks in the last box and said, 'Where's his computer?'

'I'm using it right now. Mine's been in the shop a week.' He sounded defensive: it seemed reasonable to me.

'Notice anything interesting on the hard disk?' I asked.

'No.'

I could look myself: I could hunt through the floppies. I didn't get the feeling Carl would like that, or maybe even allow it. I wouldn't push it, for now. Jams could, if it was necessary later.

I picked up the final unsearched object, the empty holdall, and began running my fingers along the seams and under the stiffened card lining the bottom. Carl was watching me intently. 'Alex—' he said. He sounded husky.

'Hang on,' I said. 'I think I've found something.' It was small, button-shaped, stuck just at the reach of a fingertip. I prodded it, wiggled my finger, tipped up the bag hoping to shake it free. It didn't budge. 'Have you got a screwdriver? Or a pair of scissors? This is stuck.'

'What is it?'

'I don't know. A button?'

'Give it here.' He took the bag, went into the front room and moved about. I started pushing the boxes back under the bed.

He came back with the bag and, on the palm of his hand, a button. A black plastic shirt button. 'There you go. Is it a clue?'

I took it, turned it over. 'Hardly,' I said.

'Then you're finished here?'

'Yes.'

'Please come and eat with me. Please. I know a really good little Italian place, and I want to get to know you better.'

We went to his little Italian place which would never, unless it sacked the chef and the singing waiter, expand into a big Italian place. We exchanged the kind of edited and glamorized highlights about ourselves that you do with someone whose bones you want to jump, and then went back to his apartment and, by midnight, there was precious little of me that he didn't know. Physically, that is.

And by midnight I wanted to leave, profoundly. I was feeling bad because, although I'd never made any promises to Barty, I knew he wouldn't like it if he knew where I was and what I'd been doing. And because Carl was involved, however indirectly, with a case, so he was not only a bit on the side but an unethical bit on the side. And because I really wasn't interested in Carl Nabokov, and he was trying so hard to be nice. He'd given me his all, pleasurably, twice, and now he was cuddling me, complimenting me and telling me about his feelings and his childhood.

Most women would have been delighted, I suppose, that he wasn't snoring and hogging the duvet. I'd have preferred it if he had, because then I could slip away leaving a note, and wrestle with my guilt alone.

As it was I lay supine, smelling his skin – musky, at first delicious, now over-sweet – and rationalized for Europe. I hadn't behaved really badly because: 1) I'd never see him again 2) I was abroad, and everyone knew abroad didn't count 3) I'd made it clear that I already had a regular lover 4) he'd used condoms, of course.

'What do you think? Hey, Alex, what do you think?'

I had no idea. When I tuned him out he'd been talking about Miss Maclellan, his inspirational high school English teacher, who sounded like a self-indulgent power-freak who'd shortly be featured in a made-for-TV biopic. He couldn't want my opinion of her.

'Sorry, Carl, I didn't hear.'

'How about we get together again?'

'I'm not likely to be in Chicago for a while.'

'Not here. In London. I'm flying over Thursday, for six weeks, to work at the British Library. Isn't that great?'

It was deeply ungreat. I didn't quite say so, but nearly. Not nearly enough: he didn't get the message. And he already had my London telephone number, on my card. And then we discovered that we were going to be on the same Thursday flight.

He was pleased. I suppose it served me right.

Wednesday, 30 March

Chapter Eight

I was due to meet Barty for breakfast in the Blackstone Grill at eight-thirty.

I always liked breakfast. I wasn't so mad on meeting Barty because I swung between fearing that a scarlet letter might appear on my forehead, and thinking that it was nothing to do with him if I chose to go to bed with someone else. The conflict made me irritable, as did the guilt. But I knew the only way not to let him suspect what I was feeling was not to feel it myself, so while I dressed I concentrated on Jacob and the case.

Then I rang Jams.

Her little-girl voice was flat, resigned, even before I'd told her what I knew. She listened in silence. Then she said, 'He told me about Carl Nabokov. His best friend. Jacob taught him for the exam.'

'*Jacob* taught him? What exam?'

'An oral thing, where they have to answer questions on books. Lots of books. Jacob knew them all, because he'd been to Oxford, and Carl didn't. So he taught him. It was the first real friend he'd ever had.'

'That's good,' I said, although it struck me that twenty-six was a bit late for your first real friend, and that Carl hadn't seen the relationship in the same way. He'd thought he'd been doing Jacob a favour. Maybe Jacob's lack of social skills led him to misinterpret. Or maybe Carl had been trying to impress me: he was the cool one, extending a streetwise hand to the isolated nerd.

'Jacob was a giver,' said Jams. 'He said he liked to give. What was hard was finding the right people to take. Anyway . . . Thanks, Alex. What are you going to do now?'

'Follow it up in England. Go to the London hotel Carl says he was staying at. Go up to his address in Doncaster.'

'But you don't expect to find him alive, do you?'

'He could be.'

'He could be. But you don't think he is.'

'I don't know what to think.'

She was crying. I could hear the sniffs. 'You're being tactful,' she said. 'I'm sure he's dead, and so are you.'

I wasn't sure of much except that Jacob's disappearance wasn't simple, and neither was Jacob himself. So I said nothing, and listened to her sniffs. 'I'm back in my flat in London on Saturday,' she said finally. 'I'll ring you then.'

'Take care,' I said.

'Why?' she said, and rang off.

So by the time I sat down in the corner booth behind the door of the coffee-shop that I'd come to think of as mine, Jams and Jacob filled my mind, insofar as I have one until I've properly woken up. Barty wasn't there yet. As usual, I ordered two eggs over easy because they didn't have blueberry muffins, and come to think of it Spenser always made his own, and dived into my first cup of coffee.

A foursome in the booth behind me were talking, loudly. They had sharp accents, like buzz-saws. I wished I could place US accents: New York everyone knew and Deep South was unmissable, mostly because it took them a decade to finish a sentence, but otherwise—

This lot were a family. Father and mother, early sixties. Daughter and son-in-law, late thirties. Middle-class, neatly dressed, the children as from Lands' End, the mother in a dress and jacket, the father in a drip-dry beige suit and open-neck white shirt. They were talking about the past. A football game.

The father was talking. 'Fran danced, that day. He threw that ball. He danced all over the field . . .'

Barty arrived, and sat down, in his visiting-Chicago expensive casual clothes, looking his usual self. He isn't good-looking – his face is too bony and Irish for that – but he always looks distinguished. Tall, rangy, tough and self-assured.

He ordered scrambled eggs and bacon and asked how I'd got on with Carl. I told him.

They were still reliving the football game, behind me, in what sounded like a script by Arthur Miller.

'I think I have a photograph of it . . . It was ridiculous, twenty bucks a ticket – we were so high up, I tell you birds were flying lower than us. We were on the oblique . . !

Then I noticed something. A smell. Of aftershave. From Barty.

He normally wears aftershave, but very little. Certainly not enough to cut through the powerful coffee-shop smell of frying bacon and weary grease.

I sniffed again. It must be him, because it was Trumper's special, the elite Curzon Street barber's own brand. I'd cleaned round the bottle on my bathroom shelf often enough.

So I looked more closely at Barty. He seemed distracted and tense, though a casual observer wouldn't have noticed because he's very controlled.

I liked him too much to duck it. 'What's the matter, Barty?' I said.

He put down his cup, cleared his throat and said, 'Alex, will you marry me?'

I hadn't been expecting that. Not then. I'd thought some extra-sensory perception of his, or just experience, had told him that I'd spent the previous night rolling about in bed with Carl, so I was knocked sideways. A bit guilty, a bit annoyed at the timing, a bit pleased. More than a bit pleased.

But I had no idea what to say, and the silence lengthened, to accommodate our neighbours' voices.

'You lived in Freeport, then, didn't you? We were in Rockford, weren't we? We could have been in Bloomington . . . That was 1980 . . . Oh, cut off of it . . . We went to Davenport 1970 . . . We had seven days to find a house and we made an offer on the sixth . . . I never liked that house . . .'

Barty was looking at me. I had to say something, so I said 'Why?'

'Because I love you. Because I want us to have children. Because I'm forty-five next birthday.'

The waitress topped up my coffee. I spooned sugar in, and stirred it. 'I think I love you too,' I said. 'But I don't know.'

'What don't you know?'

'I don't know anything, much.'

He laughed. 'Be specific. It's not like you to be girlish.'

'I'm not being girlish. I'm trying to be honest. I don't know if I want to settle down. I don't know if I want children. I don't know if I love you enough.' I didn't want future breakfasts stretching out in front of us in which I wasn't mentioning the person I'd been to bed with the night before.

I also didn't want to be the lesser partner. He had more money, more power, more education, more experience, more class. His brother was an Earl, for heaven's sake. I'd hardly fit in to his family, would I? And my children would also be his, so they'd belong to his family as well. Maybe they'd grow up to look down on me, in Little England where the classes are still just about where they were when Moses came down from the mountain carrying the tablets of stone with the orders of precedence for the second and subsequent sons of a Marquis chiselled on them.

The family behind me was leaving. Those

marriages had hung on. They must have thought it was worth it, even through all the moving about and the football games and Fran dancing, whoever Fran was. Maybe they'd managed to hang on because they were moving about. Whereas Barty and I and our children would live in Notting Hill, because no way was I going to move to the country. We'd live in Notting Hill and I'd go to bed with one man and I'd be Barty's wife—

'Do you want to talk about it?' he said.

'Not now.'

'Do you want time to think about it?'

'Yes.'

'Why?'

No reason. Every reason. Because I didn't want to commit myself and I didn't want to lose him either.

A half-truth was the best I could manage. 'I need to find out who my father was, first. In case of the children. I haven't exactly got the greatest bloodline. My mother's a schizophrenic, remember. And she's got Alzheimer's.'

'I know,' he said quietly, 'and I'm sorry, but I don't want to marry your mother, still less your father.'

'I need to know, first.'

'Are you sure you mean that?'

'Of course I'm sure,' I said snappily, because I wasn't.

'If that's what you want. Just don't make it a shroud of Laertes job.'

I didn't know what that meant, but I didn't let on. I gave the sort of reference-recognition smile that I thought would cover it, and responded to the obvious sense. 'I'll make it quick. When I've finished with Jacob. Can we talk about it again then?'

'OK.' He stretched out his hand, took mine and squeezed it. I like his touch. It's strong and familiar and exciting, and comforting too. It isn't the touch of the young Robert Mitchum, but then again, now, neither is Robert Mitchum's. And Barty wouldn't tell me about his high school English teacher.

I owed him something, and I wanted to give something, but I didn't know what. Honesty? 'Barty, I'm afraid. I don't want things to change. I don't want us to change. I don't want the future to have arrived, and the door to shut behind us.'

He was still holding my hand, and he spoke gently. 'Honey, if you don't want to change, I've bad news. You were born in the wrong species on the wrong planet. Here on Earth, things change, all the time. But sometimes it's for the better. And sometimes doors shut to keep bad things out.'

I nodded. He could work that lot up into a post-trauma counselling session, no problem.

He gave my hand a last squeeze, and let it go. 'What do you want to do today, joy of my life?' he said.

'Get a plane home. I don't want to wait till tomorrow. There's a hotel in Bayswater I want to visit. And oh, Barty – the loop.'

'What about it?'

'What could it mean?'

'The area just north of here?'

'Apart from that.'

'Hangman's noose. Loop the loop, in an aeroplane. Loopy-crazy. Mispronouncing the French for wolf. A nickname from the Spanish name, Lupe. A dubbing loop, for sound. The inner circle of a decision-making process – a president, Bush I think, said he was "outside the loop". You really should give me a context.'

'Something Jacob said to Jams. "The real me is in the loop." '

'He could feel he's being throttled by something. His childhood, perhaps?'

'You think it's metaphorical.'

'Just guessing,' he said.

Thursday, 31 March

Chapter Nine

The taxi from Heathrow dropped me at my flat just after ten. I waved Barty off and stood on the pavement, glad to be home. It was a beautiful London morning: cool, clear, sunny. Very good weather, this spring. Global warming?

I could hear the hum of the computer as soon as I opened the door of my first-floor maisonette, which meant my assistant Nick was there. Good. I'd called the day before to see if she'd be free: she wasn't always, because she wasn't always my assistant either. Officially, she's a student at a local college, coming up for her A level examinations, due to go to medical school in September. I'd taken her on for work experience a while back because my ex-social worker, who was also hers, asked me to. Nick was sleeping on the streets at the time and because she wasn't eighteen yet she was officially in care.

She's still sleeping on the streets when she isn't crashing with Grace Macarthy. No way am I going to let her stay at my place. But she helps me out when she doesn't have to turn up at college (which is most of the time, because she's very bright) and when she

isn't working with a very old, half-batty, half-brilliant
Oxford mathematician she'd met on one of my cases.
I even pay her, sometimes, because she's useful.

Particularly for the 'missing kid' side of the business. More children than you'd believe go missing, all
the time. Most of them because they can't stand it at
home. And many of them come to the London streets,
where Nick swims like an unthreatened fish. And
many of the kids' parents, driven by guilt or anger or
maybe just love, want to find them, and are prepared
to pay.

Nick handles all that, now. It'll be a dent in my
income when she leaves.

I also can't do without her at present because I've
just installed a new PC, on her advice, and until I get
the hang of e-mail and the Internet, she'll stay on the
payroll.

She didn't leave the computer when I came into
the room. She hardly even looked up. 'Hi,' she said.
'This is the last of the invoices. Coffee just made, in
the kitchen.'

'Hi, Nick. All well?'

She didn't answer. With most people, she's an elec-
tive mute, and even with me she doesn't produce con-
ventional small-talk responses. A restful quality in an
assistant.

I took a mug of coffee and looked over her
shoulder at the reassuringly high figures in the
invoice on the screen. My business is doing well. If I
married Barty, who's a good earner himself and who
also has (by my estimate) a solid chunk of capital, I'd

be better off still. And my children would have a good start.

And, to be fair to Barty, I'd have to treat the search for my father as just another case: handle it quickly, in other words. Start handling it now.

The obvious place to start was with my ex-social worker, who'd dealt with me since I was four. I reached for the telephone.

No luck at her office. I tried her mobile.

'Hello.'

'Mary? This is Alex Tanner.'

Nick shied away from me like a nervous horse and started making 'I'm not here' gestures. I made 'nothing-to-do-with-you' faces back, and she calmed down.

'Alex! How nice to hear from you! Is this about Nick?' said Mary warmly. She says everything warmly, it's her job.

'No. Nick's fine, as far as I know.' Nick gave me a 'thumbs-up', sat back down at the PC, and set the printer running. 'It's about me. I'm thinking of getting married.'

Nick was now miming 'Are you mad?' She's gay, and she has a very low opinion of men, mostly because her mother was a prostitute and partly because she's met some crap men.

I ignored her. Mary was congratulating me supportively and professionally, though she's not mad on men either. Her male lover left her for a male probation officer. I let Mary run for a while, then interrupted. 'Yeah, thanks, but the thing is, I want to find my father.'

Mary rambled on about it being an important decision, about the need for counselling, about an understanding colleague who was well qualified in this very area, though with the cutbacks in Government funding—

'Sure, Mary. I don't want counselling, though. I want facts. Do you know who he is? My mother said he was a taxi-driver she met in a pub. Is that true?'

More rambling. Nick was now folding the invoices and stuffing them into envelopes, without looking at me.

'So you don't? My mother never told you?'

Supportive ramble.

'I know she was off her head. But that was only most of the time. In the windows of sanity, did she never say?'

Ramble.

'So you have no idea?'

Silence. Then – 'No. Sorry, Alex. No idea.'

I rang off.

Nick said, 'Anything you want processed, now I'm on the machine?'

I pointed to my carry-on holdall. 'Type up the notes in the blue folder, labelled "Drugs doc".'

She rifled through the holdall, pulled out the folder. A plastic bag came with it and spilled its contents on the carpet. My freebie plunder. She looked at it, then at me. 'Can I?' she said.

She'd taken to doing this when I came back from

trips abroad. I nodded. She spread it out and looked at the little packages. 'Toothbrush and toothpaste?'

'Airline.'

'Slippers?'

'Airline.'

'Soap? Shower gel?'

'Hotel.'

'Salt and pepper and sugar?'

'Eateries.'

She stirred the gleaming little pile with her finger, and then I tumbled to something I should have done five trips ago. 'It's for you,' I said.

'D'you mean it?'

'Yes.'

She gathered them up, put them back in the plastic bag, put the bag in her carrier. 'Thank you.'

'You're welcome,' I said, feeling the ground shift under my feet. In a second I'd gone from being the little girl who has to steal her own treats because she's underparented, to the adult who consoles the left-behind child by collecting tiny tokens of affection as they roam the world.

At present, I didn't like it. I'd better get used to it, I thought, looking yearningly at the empty carpet where my small reassurances had been. Grow up, Alex. It's time.

So I went to have a bath. Back to the womb. Really grown up.

When I came back down to the living-room, Nick had gone, probably to take the invoices to the post.

It was eleven o'clock: plenty of the working day

left. I'd slept on the plane and, for the moment, was raring to go.

I listened to the messages on the answering machine. Some upcoming work, which I noted.

Polly burbling on about arriving on Friday and looking forward to seeing me. As usual, she talked for too long and was cut off in mid-sentence, but I noted her flight arrival time. If I could, I'd meet her at Heathrow: I was using her car and had been for the last few months, so it was the least I could do.

Alan Protheroe, who I'd rung from Chicago and left a message for the day before, fussing about why I was coming back one day early and what was wrong and he hoped I wasn't expecting to be paid for the full three days and would I get in touch, please, immediately.

Alan always fusses. I'd ring him tomorrow.

His was the last message.

Still no sign of Nick.

I took a half-mug of lukewarm coffee and sat back down at the phone. I owed it to Barty to keep pressing on for my father, although I didn't want to, I increasingly realized. I really didn't want to know. I hadn't wanted to know for my whole lifetime, otherwise I'd have pursued it with my mother before she finally retreated into the limbo of advanced Alzheimer's disease.

Why didn't I want to know? Why hadn't I thought about it? I'm curious by nature and as much of a navel-gazer as the next sucker who always does 'know-yourself' quizzes in trash magazines.

I sipped the coffee and tried to face the fact that I didn't even want to know why I didn't want to know. Just thinking about it made me feel empty and insubstantial and ill.

Jet-lag, I said to myself firmly, and picked up the phone.

I got lucky on my third number. 'Eddy? Alex Tanner. How's my favourite policeman?'

'Your only policeman, you mean,' said Eddy. His voice, like him, was simultaneously genial and faintly threatening. He's a successful detective of the old school, a thief-taker, and an even more successful ladies' man. He's a superintendent in the Metropolitan Police, and though he's very able he'll never rise any higher because his idea of community relations is to bang up males and bang females. He's an old family friend and the father of my first serious boyfriend and I use him unmercifully.

'What can I do you for?' he said. 'I presume this isn't a social call, and if it is I'm too busy, so sod off.'

'Eddy, do you know who my father is?'

Silence. Then, cautiously: 'Why are you asking?'

Silence my end. I'd had an astonishing thought. 'Eddy, should I call you Dad?' He's always spoilt me, but I'd assumed that was just because he liked kids and we got on. But maybe—

'Put that idea right out of your mind, girl. Right out. Me and your mum were close, yeah, but that was after you were born. Well after. Otherwise there's no way I'd have let you go out with young Peter. Or made passes at you.'

'Of course not,' I said. 'So, can you help me out on this?'

'Why do you want to know?'

'Why don't you want to tell me?'

'I've got to think.'

'You? Think?'

'You free around noon tomorrow?'

'Could be.'

'Meet me in the Churchill for a bevvy, we'll talk about it,' he said, and rang off.

It wasn't like him to be delicate, or discreet. What was he playing at? Maybe my father was a serial killer. Or the Commissioner of the Metropolitan Police.

And I had to wait until tomorrow to find out.

My heart was already doing flip-flops from the second or so when I'd guessed I was Eddy's child. I'm not enjoying this, I thought.

Key in the lock. Nick was back. 'I've posted the invoices,' she said, then looked at me closely. 'What's the matter?'

'Jet-lag,' I said. 'Forget it. We're off out on a new case. A misper, your favourite. I'll tell you about it in the car.'

Chapter Ten

The Saxe-Coburg Hotel, Jacob's last address, was in Bayswater, just west of Queensway, about ten minutes drive from my flat. It spread along three socking great stucco-fronted Victorian terraced houses. It was lower range, package-tour country. I found a meter fifty yards away, fed it ludicrous sums of money – parking in London is beyond a joke – and set off for the hotel, threading my way through the piles of luggage and swarms of middle-aged tourists in sensible walking shoes that had just been deposited by a huge air-conditioned German coach.

I was nearly there before I realized that Nick, who I'd told to stay in the car, was beside me.

I stopped. 'What's this, Nick?'

'I want to come with you.'

'Why?'

She shrugged, expressionless. She's nearly always expressionless. She's half-Asian and about twice as inscrutable as most whole Asians I've known. She's almost as inscrutable as Barty, when he wants to be.

'OK,' I said. 'Get your cap from the car.' The top of her scalp is bare in patches, where she's pulled her hair out. If she wears a baseball cap the patches don't show, and she doesn't frighten the punters.

I waited. When she came back presentable, she said, 'You went away to America.'

'And?'

'I missed you.'

Sometimes she regresses. I ignore it. 'OK, let's get in before the tourists. Just don't speak, all right?'

She nodded, scornfully.

Inside, the hotel was cleanish, uglyish and anonymous. Unless Jacob had really distinguished himself, by doing a runner without paying his bill or assaulting a maid, I didn't expect anyone to remember him.

I was pleased to see someone was manning the Enquiries desk while three girls dealt with the long queue at check-in, otherwise we'd have been there all night, and even more pleased when I saw what he was like. He was probably in his early thirties but he looked fifty and a drinker. He had a puffy face, red eyes, a too-loose, too-blue suit and grubby hands. A plaque on the desk told me he was James O'Reilly, Assistant Manager.

A direct approach. 'Good morning, Mr O'Reilly. I'm a private investigator,' I said. 'Here's my credentials.' I gave him a business card and twenty quid.

He gave them straight back. 'Are you serious?' he said in a sharp East End voice.

'Perfectly serious,' I said, and added another twenty.

The money vanished, the card remained on his desk. 'Well, Alex Tanner, what you want?'

'I was told a man called Jacob Stone stayed here September last year. Can you check that for me?'

He clicked away at the keyboard beside him, looked at the result on the screen, and nodded.

'Yup,' he said.

'Yup what?'

'Yup, he stayed here.'

I walked round behind the desk and looked at the display on the monitor. It was the seating plan for a dental hygienists' convention dinner to be held next month.

'Give me my credentials back,' I said. 'Or show me something useful.'

'Nasty suspicious mind you've got,' he said, not offended, not even irritated.

'It's a requirement in my line of work.'

'What date in September are we talking?'

'After the twenty-fifth.'

'I'll have to go through day by day.'

'So start.'

He started while I watched. Nick propped herself against a would-be decorative pillar and tried to keep her hands from drifting up to tug at her hair. She'd obviously been much more stressed than I realized by my very short trip, or maybe it was the prospect of my marriage, I suddenly thought, because I'd worked away before since I'd known her and for longer periods too. I smiled at her and she turned her head away.

'Here you are. Jacob Stone. Stayed for three days, September 27th to 30th. Paid in cash.'

I looked at Jacob's receipted bill glowing away on the screen. He'd been there, he'd stayed. He hadn't used room service or the telephone – damn, because I'd have got the numbers – he'd paid, he'd left. According to Carl, he hadn't been there when Carl had looked, the second day of his stay and he hadn't responded to messages Carl had left. He just might not have wanted to, of course. Maybe he was too busy with something else.

What?

That was a speculation for later.

'Did he leave a forwarding address?'

O'Reilly just laughed.

'The hotel wouldn't have kept it?'

He laughed again.

'What address did he put in the register?'

'That's a legal document. You can't look at that.'

'But you can.'

I expected him to ask for more money, but he just shrugged and went through a door at the side of the reception area. I looked at Nick but she looked away.

O'Reilly came back with a slip of paper. *Ormskirk Drive, Armthorpe, Doncaster.* Stone's home address from Oxford days.

The next stop.

Back in the car, I entered O'Reilly's bribe in my expenses for Jams.

'What now?' said Nick.

'Now I go to Doncaster.' I didn't feel tired yet; if I

did, later, I could always stay at a motel up north and drive back in the morning. Nick could get on with typing up my notes and invoice for Alan.

'Where's that?'

'Up north. Towards Leeds.'

'What's that?'

'A major city in the North. Half-way to Scotland.' She was great on maths and science, not so good on basic geography, apart from the London streets.

'How long will it take?'

'Three hours and a bit.'

'Will you eat at a motorway service place?'

'Maybe, if I'm really hungry. Why?'

'I've never been on a motorway,' she said, looking straight in front of her and twisting the baseball cap in her hands. 'I've never eaten at a motorway service place.'

She hadn't missed anything. 'Do you want to come with me?'

'Yeah,' she said. Her face would have lit up if it had been the sort of face that could. 'I could drive, some of the way.'

'But you can't drive.'

'Sure I can. I've been joyriding since I was eight.'

'No way. No licence, no drive. Not in Polly's car. She'd have fifty fits.'

'I don't like Polly,' she said, with a spurt of undirected, threatened malice.

'You've never met her. Save your opinion till tomorrow. She's coming for the weekend. You can judge for yourself.' I started the car and drove.

'You're going back to the flat,' she said, several streets later.

'Yeah. We've got to pick up some stuff, in case we stay up north overnight.'

'Then we'll eat at a motorway service place?'

'If you want. The food's rubbish.'

'I'll judge for myself,' she said, and grinned.

Chapter Eleven

The land around Doncaster was very flat. Flat fields, as far as the eye could see, which was pretty far. There were pitheads and electricity pylons striding to the horizon, and power stations with their drifting white trails of steam; some leafy suburbs and outlying neighbourhoods, once villages but now part of the sprawling town, with rows of small terraced houses, and above it all, the stunning sky, high and blue and laced with scudding clouds. Up here it was windy.

Nick had read through all my Jacob Stone notes, when she wasn't nagging me to stop for food or coffee, and now she was map-reading. We reached Armthorpe just after five. It was a small ex-mining town: corner shops, video shops, cut-price supermarkets, a pit-head in the town itself, and plenty of little houses.

Although I knew the north was in recession, and had been in recession for years, they seemed to be weathering it well. The houses were well-kept with clean curtains, new doors and spruce gardens.

We asked our way to Ormskirk Drive, and the natives were friendly. Plenty of 'me loves' and 'me ducks', plus workable directions which took us to a narrow residential street of very small houses with a busy adolescent-hangout chippy at one end and a large brick building which announced itself as a Rugby League drinking club at the other.

A long way from Christ Church College, Oxford, I thought as I parked the Golf outside the unoccupied-looking, curtained windows of Number 5. He'd gone home every weekend. That'd have cost money which, judging from the house, his family didn't have. What was he going home for? Not luxury. Affection possibly, the fierce affection of the fierce woman in the graduation photograph. Familiarity, possibly. He felt out of his depth in Oxford.

But he'd chosen to make an academic career. He wanted it enough to work and save for it, in a job and a world he hated, according to Jams.

'This it?' said Nick, peering past me at the house. 'It doesn't look like he's here.'

It didn't look like anyone was there, or had been for some months. The rose-bushes in the three-foot front garden were straggling unpruned, old fish-and-chip wrappers caught in their branches.

'I'll try anyway,' I said.

I got out and went up to the door. Nick followed me. I looked for a bell but there wasn't one, so I used the door-knocker, brass, once-polished, now dull. It sounded loud in my own ears. A curtain twitched at the front window of the next house along.

I knocked again, not expecting an answer, then peered in to the front room. It was an old-fashioned parlour. Very old-fashioned. A scrubbed plank floor with rag rugs, wooden furniture, oil lamps. No comfortable chairs, no padding, no ornaments. Plenty of old hard-backed books, the kind that looked as if they'd have yellowed, speckled pages and smell of damp.

The next-door curtain twitched again. I was being Neighbourhood Watched. I moved to the curtain-twitching house. The door was opened before I rang by a middle-aged woman, my height but well over my weight class, wearing a purple and black print cotton dress underneath a blue overall. 'Can I help you, me duck?' she said.

I was sure she could. Under her tight perm she had eager prying eyes in a round face which had Nosy written all over it.

'Hi,' I said. 'I'm Alex Tanner, a private investigator looking for Jacob Stone. I was hoping to find him here.' I gave her a card and she read it, excited.

'Oooh – a private investigator. I've never seen one of them off the telly. Maggie Whittaker, pleased to meet you. Who's he, your bodyguard?' She nodded at Nick, who was standing by the car. She was wearing jeans and a heavy denim shirt; she's tall, flat-chested, broad-shouldered, narrow-hipped: people had mistaken her for a boy before and I considered not putting Mrs Nosy right, in case it alienated her, then decided it would alienate her more if she found out later.

'He's a she, my assistant, Nick Straker.'

'Hiya, love, sorry about that, my eyes aren't what they were. Have you come far?'

'From London.'

'You'll be wanting a drink, then, and the toilet. Come in, both of you.'

The front room was small and spanking clean, with rose-patterned wallpaper and a new bright pink three-piece suite that occupied most of the available floor-space. Like Carl's bed in his bedroom, I thought. Carl would be leaving for the airport now, on his way to London. I'd made a big mistake with Carl. But I'd be making a bigger mistake if I didn't concentrate because I was brooding about it, so I sipped my tea enthusiastically, smiled at Maggie Whittaker, and admired the furniture. Nick sat beside me, crouched up defensively, her tea cooling on a side table.

'D'you mind if I tape our conversation?' I said, taking out my little cassette recorder.

'Of course not. Who'll you play it to?' she said.

'Only us. To check if we've forgotten anything.'

'Oh. Well, that's OK with me,' said Maggie, much less Yorkshire. 'So what's your business with Jacob?'

'My client is worried about him. He seems to have disappeared.'

'Who's your client?'

'His fiancée.'

'I didn't know he was walking out with a girl,' she said.

More standing up and pumping, I thought. 'She's a model,' I said. 'A leg model.'

'Oooh,' she said. 'Would I know her to look at?'

'You'd know her legs. She's the Sheer Heaven girl.'

'Oooh. On the poster down by Presto.'

'That's the one.'

'He's done well for himself,' she said. 'I always knew he'd do well for himself. A serious boy, not like some of the others round here.'

'She hasn't heard from him since last September. He was supposed to ring her, but he hasn't, and he isn't at college in America.'

'I haven't seen him to talk to since his mother's funeral,' she said. 'He went back to America then, to Chicago. You know his mother died?'

'Yes, I'm sorry about Mrs Stone,' I said. 'Was she a friend of yours?'

'It *was* sad, but we wasn't close. Not since we was kids at school together. I knew Janet well then, but not after she married Zeke Stone. They kept themselves to themselves, being Tubbies, of course.'

'Tubbies?'

'The church in t'next road. Christ's Children of the Fountain of the Water of Life.'

'Why do you call them Tubbies?'

'D'you know, I'm not reet sure? That's what we call 'em, always have.'

'Tubmaster,' said Nick. It was the first word she'd spoken in Maggie Whittaker's hearing, and the woman smiled at her encouragingly.

'What's that, me love?'

'In your notes, Alex,' said Nick, ignoring her. 'Jacob's research. Thomas Tubmaster, who founded a sect. This must be it.'

'Happen,' said Maggie, who was getting more York-shire by the second. 'Aye, happen.'

'So most of Mrs Stone's and Jacob's friends would be members of the church?' I said.

'That's reet.'

'Who's the minister?'

'Abraham Master. Do you want his address?'

'And telephone number, if you have it.'

'The Tubbies don't hold with telephones. Nor telly, nor any man-made fibres. Like those in the film with Harrison Ford.'

'The Amish?'

'Aye. Bit strange, but good neighbours. I'll say that for them. Abraham lives at 12 Victory Road. Turn right at chippy. If he's not at home, he'll likely be praying in t'chapel next door. Is there owt wrong with the tea, me duck?'

Nick looked at Maggie, looked at me, then drank her tea like a medicine. I nudged her. 'Thank you,' she said. No social skills, but a sharp assistant, though I'd have spotted Tubmaster myself, eventually. Maybe age was slowing me up. Or maybe it was Carl.

I made the withdrawing you've-been-very-helpful noises. Maggie was still holding my card. 'I'll call you, will I, if I hear owt about Jacob?'

'Please do.'

We were on the way to the car when Maggie caught up with us. 'You could try Sandra.'

'Sandra?'

'Janet's sister. Sandra Balmer.'

'Does she live around here?'

'Not round here. Gone up in the world. I'll get the address for you . . .'

Quickly, she was back with a scrap of paper. 'There you go. She may not speak to you – she's a mind of her own – and she and Janet fell out a while back, so she may not be able to help you even if she wanted to, but there's not much goes on that Sandra doesn't stick her nose into. It's worth a go.'

Chapter Twelve

There was no answer when I knocked on the door of Abraham Master's house, so I went next door to the chapel, as Maggie'd advised.

The Church of the Fountain of the Water of Life was a square grey-stone building, about a hundred feet by a hundred by sixty high, with one row of narrow plain glass windows in each side, near the roof, almost like skylights. It was set back from the road and stood apart from the late-Victorian red-brick terraced houses on either side. It looked as if it had been there first which, if it was Tubmaster's original eighteenth-century foundation, it certainly had. It was surrounded by a low stone wall enclosing a grav-elled area. There was a gap in the centre of the wall facing the street, and from it a flagged path led to big black wooden double doors in the centre of the chapel on the street side.

A large board mounted on a wooden post beside the gap was lettered in gold paint with the name of the church and the minister, and a text: Revelation 22, LET HIM WHO IS THIRSTY COME, LET HIM WHO DESIRES TAKE

THE WATER OF LIFE WITHOUT PRICE. I hoped they'd be equally generous with information.

I stood in the street for a moment, wondering what struck me as odd about the church. Then I clicked. It was in good repair. The roof looked sound, the stone had recently been cleaned, the windows gleamed and the doors and noticeboard were freshly painted.

Peculiar, for what must surely be a dwindling congregation in a large and expensive-to-maintain structure? Unless the minister was so charismatic that Tubbies flocked from far and wide to hang on his words, and gave the church all the money their lifestyle saved them on cars and electricity bills and telephone bills and computers and TVs and rental videos – on living in the 1990s, in fact.

I waved at Nick, who I'd left in the car to locate Sandra Balmer's address on the map, mimed 'won't be long', and went past the poster, up the path, through the doors (which I'd half expected not to be open) and into the building.

It was a cavernous space. The windows only admitted a fraction of the light still lingering outside, and it was otherwise only lit by several tall, presumably oil-burning, brass lampstands. Row upon row of plain wooden chairs stretched into the gloom – upwards of three hundred, I guessed.

Only the front two rows were occupied, by about forty people, with a scattering of very small children but mostly middle-aged or older, dressed in black and white. They were standing to pray, facing a bare table with a large book on a wooden stand. I couldn't make out what they were mumbling, but the tone was intense and self-righteous.

At each corner of the chairs, facing outwards as if on guard, stood a man clutching a tall, antique weapon. A pike?

When the guards heard me they all turned to face me and then the two nearest ones started to move in my direction in a slow heavy-stamping ceremonial march.

I stood and waited.

When they reached me, they stood side by side facing me about four feet apart and lowered their pikes towards each other so the weapons formed an X barring my way.

They were both wearing black rough-looking serge trousers tucked in to long black leather boots, white collarless shirts and long black waistcoats, the sort of all-purpose 'not-contemporary' costumes the RSC use for minor characters. They both had very close-cropped hair. Right was fortyish, tall, red-faced and solid. Left was younger, medium height, pale-faced and even more solid. Dressed differently, neither of them would have been out of place in a tag-wrestling contest.

'Halt!' said Right.

Since I was already standing still, I did nothing, not knowing my lines and rather sorry to be spoiling their fun.

'I am a Squarekeeper,' he said. 'Do you seek the destruction of Christ's Children?'

That reminded me of the U.S. Immigration forms which ask if you intend to overthrow the government. 'No,' I said.

'Are you a seeker after truth?'

I was, but not in the way he meant. 'I wanted to speak to Abraham Master,' I said.

'The Squarekeeper General is at prayer.'

'Will he be taking a break soon? When this prayer ends, for instance?'

Right and Left both curled their lips contemptuously. 'Our prayers do not end,' said Left.

As he spoke, the congregation fell silent and sat down. They'd ignored me throughout, but now one of them left the front row and came over to me.

He was in his late thirties, medium height and muscular, with balding fair hair and a soft-looking face with wet lips. He wore a dark suit, cheap and shiny, a white shirt and a dog-collar.

When he reached us Left and Right marched in place and banged the bottom of their pikes on the flagged floor. He saluted, they presented arms and stood still.

'A seeker after truth, Master,' said Right.

'Back to your posts,' said the man I supposed was Abraham Master, although I now saw it was probably not a name but a title, the guards stamped away and we were left facing each other.

I apologized for the interruption and told him who I was and what I wanted. He turned the card I'd given him over and over in his hands, then put it in his pocket.

'Return on Monday,' he said. 'I will speak to you then.'

'Monday?'

'This is Holy Week, sister. In Holy Week we must pray, and we do no secular business, only God's work.'

'But . . .'

'Only God's work. Until He is risen. I will talk to you on Monday, not before. Christ keep you.' He left me and went back to the congregation.

I went into the air and fading sunlight with relief, and stood on the path outside, thinking. This religion was seriously weird. Armed guards. Funny titles. No decoration, no statues, no organ for music. The church had been too warm, heated by four large new-looking wood-burning stoves, one in the centre of each wall, but it had also smelt damp and old and left-behind. Anything less like the source of the Water of Life I couldn't imagine.

But it did help me to understand Jacob. Now I could see why he could have lived for a year in International House. Barrack-like, impersonal: familiar to someone who must have spent much of his childhood praying here. 'An ordinary home,' he'd said. Denial? Wishful thinking? Rejection? He must have rejected the church to some extent because it could hardly be in line with Tubmaster's moral teaching to have carnal knowledge of a leg model. And a Tubby surely shouldn't have been in an aircraft in the first place.

*

'How'd it go?' said Nick, when I rejoined her in the car.

'He was there, but he won't talk to me until after Easter.'

'When's that?'

'Sunday. I'll have to come back on Monday.'

'*We'll* have to,' she said pointedly.

'Maybe.'

'So what do we do now?'

It was six o'clock, and I wasn't tired yet. 'How long will it take us to get to Sandra Balmer's place? Have you found it?'

'I've got the village – only about ten miles away. I tried Directory Enquiries for a phone number, but she's ex-directory.'

'Where'd you find a phone?'

'Round the corner, outside the chippy. I'm not quite brainless, you know. And it's time you got a mobile, I can't work under these conditions. I'm hungry. Can I have some fish and chips?'

'No.'

'A can of Pepsi?'

'Oh, all right.'

On the drive over to Sandra Balmer's jet-lag or just plain tiredness began to hit me. I felt as if I'd been awake for thirty hours on the trot, and I was losing interest in Jacob and everything except a hotel room and a bed that I could crash on face down, dreamlessly. I hoped that we'd find the house empty.

No such luck. We located it quickly – only had to ask directions once. It was on the outskirts of a pretty country village called Gringley-on-the-Hill. It was a bungalow which had taken a sideways growth pill and then erupted into decorative classical columns. There were plenty of lights on, glowing into the dusk from wide uncurtained windows. She answered the door-bell on my first ring, and after only the briefest of introductions Nick and I were swept inside for a sweet sherry and a chat.

The living-room was over-furnished and expens-ive: sofas and chairs of white leather, masses of pastel cushions, plenty of little tables, carpet cream-col-oured and thick, ornaments, dried-flower arrange-ments heavily scented with pot-pourri oil. There was a bar with high stools across a corner of the room and she'd fetched our sherry from a tall padded floor-to-ceiling pink leather cupboard behind it with a built-in fridge at the bottom.

The pale pink wallpaper had a stippled effect, and most of the pictures were lush sentimental land-scapes, vaguely Mediterranean – olive-groves or medieval streets leading steeply down to an improb-ably blue sea dotted with bright fishing-boats.

The temperature was Mediterranean too. The cen-tral heating was full on and superfluous gas flames licked at the imitation logs in the fireplace. The large mantelpiece was mock-marble, and above it hung the only portrait in the room. It was flattering, slightly misty, possibly done from a photograph. The subject was a distinctly attractive youngish woman with fluffy blonde hair and big wide-set blue eyes and clear white skin with a faint pink tinge about the high cheekbones, and a warm, sympathetic, understanding smile.

Sandra, the original of the portrait, was sitting opposite us – older, mid-forties at a guess, but still smiling warmly, still attractive in well-cut black wool slacks, an expensive-looking cream sweater with patterns of gold thread, and almost enough chunky gold jewellery to buy the bungalow.

'Quite comfy?' she said in a rich Yorkshire accent which must have been partly affectation because sometimes she didn't sound regional. 'More sherry?'

'We're fine, thanks,' I said, conscious of the turkish-bath sweat beginning to break out all over me and the sticky sherry sweetness coating my teeth. That was the first thing either Nick or I had said since my opening line, 'I'm a private investigator and I'd like to speak to you about Jacob Stone.' Our hostess had chattered non-stop ever since, all of it to do with our comfort, none of it to do with Jacob. I had to get on top of this or I'd fall asleep.

I switched on the tape recorder in my bag, and said, cutting across her, 'About Jacob – he's your nephew, isn't he?'

'Yes, that's right,' she said. 'And you're a private investigator? Bit of excitement for me, meeting you. Now if I had to imagine a private investigator it would be a man sitting there in a mac with a whisky bottle sticking out of a torn pocket, coughing and flicking ash on the carpet.'

'Do you mind ash on the carpet?' said Nick, and I looked at her, surprised that she'd volunteered small-talk to a stranger.

'Not really, my dear, though maybe I have got a mite fussy, living alone. Men have their little ways, don't they, and the cream isn't a practical colour and it'd have taken time to get the marks out, but then what's time for, when you come to think of it?'

She looked round the immaculate room. I looked with her, and saw time hanging heavy as cigarette smoke. There were no photographs, no books, no writing materials, no magazines, not even a television on display. If she lived alone, why choose what must be a five-bedroomed, five-bathroomed house? Did she sleep in a different room each night, and bathe in a different bath each morning, and use fresh towels each day so she could put them through the washing-machine? She could hardly be more different to her sister, I thought, remembering the graduation photo-graph, and this house was light-years from the stark-ness of Ormskirk Drive.

'About Jacob,' I said again. 'My client has hired me to find him. He's dropped out of his graduate course at Chicago and he hasn't been seen since last Sep-tember.'

'And your client is?'

'A woman friend.'

'Name of?' said Sandra warmly, picking up the sherry bottle. 'Sure I can't tempt you?'

'No, thanks,' I said firmly.

'Yes, please,' said Nick. I glared at her, and she backed down.

'The boss doesn't approve,' she said, nodding at me. 'Better not.'

'Whatever you say,' said Sandra to me, with a cosy we're-the-adults conspiratorial smile. 'I always think a nice drop of sherry never did anyone any harm, but you're the boss.'

I felt unlike the boss of anything. Sandra's fluffiness screened a very un-fluffy determination, and I was beginning to think I'd get nowhere with her. 'My client is Emily Treliving,' I said. 'The woman he was going to marry.'

'The girl he met on the plane,' said Sandra. 'She would be worried, I can see that. Men! They play fast and loose, so often, don't they? Trample all over our feelings.'

'Mrs Balmer—'

'Call me Sandra, do.'

'Sandra, have you seen Jacob since last September?'

She topped up her own glass and put the bottle down. 'Of course,' she said. 'Of course I have. And I spoke to him only last week.'

Chapter Thirteen

Now I'm pushing thirty, I must be getting sentimental. My first thought was, poor Jams. Poor, poor Jams. She'd been so sure. So sure he loved her, so sure the only reason for not hearing from him was that he was dead.

Whereas it was just a dragged-out version of the old, old story. Boy meets girl. Boy lies to girl. Girl sits by silent telephone.

My second thought was more characteristic. Let's get to the bottom of this. OK, maybe Jams had considerably overestimated the seriousness of his intentions towards her. But dropping out of his graduate course? Not the Jacob I thought I knew. 'Kinda close with his money,' Carl had said. But he paid fees in advance for a term he didn't turn up for, and he hadn't, as far as I knew, applied for a refund.

Plus, before that, he'd worked four years in a job he hated to earn enough money to make the life he wanted as a university teacher. Why would he just blow that away? A methodical man, a planner. I could see his precise, tiny writing, and hear Carl saying Jacob was, 'Very clear, very directed.' If he had changed direction, it would have been for a powerful reason.

I looked at Sandra who was smiling sympathetically, and thought irritably, if she's such a warm human being, how come she needs the heating up so high? I said, 'So Jacob's all right, is he?'

'It depends what you mean by "all right",' she said. 'He was very, very upset by his mother's death. They were close. Too close, I reckon.'

'Which could have been why he fell in love with my client,' I said, fighting the rear-guard action Jams was paying me for.

'I don't know about that, my dear,' she said. 'I think Jams Treliving is part of his problem. I'm interested – how did she find you?'

'Through a friend,' I said. 'And I happened to be in Chicago earlier in the week, so she met me there.'

'In Chicago! Really! How long were you there for?'

'I went over on Sunday and came back today.'

'All that way! For three days! With jet-lag! What a strong girl you must be!'

She'd be feeling my muscles next. I smiled politely, and said, 'So what exactly *is* his problem?'

'Too much strain. Emotional strain. Losing his mother and then making a commitment, much too quickly, to someone he'd known only a very short time.'

'Sandra, forgive me, but you've only known him a very short time as well, haven't you?'

She was taken aback. Her smile flickered and

came back again with increased wattage. 'Why do you say that?'

'I understood that you and your sister had lost touch quite a while ago. On her marriage, when she joined the Church of the Fountain of the Water of Life. You didn't know Jacob when he was growing up, did you?'

She hesitated. 'Not as such,' she said. 'I heard about him, naturally, through mutual friends. But then when he was left alone, of course he came to me.'

It didn't seem 'of course' to me at all. Jacob was twenty-six, developing his chosen career in another country. His mother dies, OK, but that would just liberate him to go back to America and carry on with his life. And if he was specially close to his mother and presumably loyal to her, he wouldn't seek out a sister she'd broken off contact with years before. 'I need to speak to him. Where is he now?' I said.

'Why do you need to speak to him?' she said.

Because I don't believe you, I thought. She'd met Jacob all right, since he came back to England – she knew two things I hadn't told her, Jams's nickname, and that Jacob had met her on a plane – but I didn't buy the rest of her story. 'I owe it to my client,' I said briskly, wiped the central-heating sweat from my writing hand on the side of my jeans and sat with pen poised over my notebook.

'That won't be possible,' she said, her voice sweetly frosted like the icing on a package-mix cake. 'He needs to be alone.'

'That's fine by me,' I said. 'He can be alone twenty-four hours a day and double time on weekends. Five minutes is all I need. Where is he?'

'In Kyrgyzstan,' she said.

'How are you spelling that?' I said, in what was probably a vain attempt to disguise the fact that I'd no idea what she'd said. Was it a country, a city, a bed and breakfast in Doncaster? Was it a well-known local dialect word for cloud-cuckoo-land?

She spelt it for me, then went on: 'I'd never heard of it, and I certainly couldn't spell it until I looked it up on a map. It's near China. He rang me from the capital a week ago. He's been travelling in the east since December. He said he needed to have time to think.'

Truth, or diversionary tactic? I didn't know. It was an unlikely invention, for her. She didn't look to me as if she'd been much further east than Marbella, nor as if she spent her over-heated evenings poring over off-the-beaten-track travel brochures. Kyrgyzstan wasn't a place that would leap to her lips, if she had to make a story up as she went along.

'And he was all right when you spoke to him?'

'More at peace, yes.'

'So why hasn't he got in touch with Jams? If he could ring you, then he could ring her.'

'He felt very badly about her. As if he'd let her down.'

'Which he had,' I said.

'Ah well. Men. They're weak, but you have to love them, don't you?' She was smiling again, like a conspirator, all-girls-together.

I didn't smile back. 'Some of them, possibly,' I said, and Nick made a 'count-me-out' face even from that. 'So you haven't *seen* Jacob since last December?'

'No. But I've spoken to him every so often since, and he was all right last week. Not perfectly happy in himself, but all right. Drawing tranquillity from the high snows. That's what he said.'

'And he's just abandoned his graduate studies?'

'I wouldn't know what his plans are. So perhaps,' she said draining her sherry glass and setting it down like a punctuation mark, 'you can tell Jams what I've told you, and set her mind at rest. Sure I can't press you to more sherry?'

Should I tell her about Jams's baby? That news would flush Jacob out, surely, and give me leverage. But I didn't trust Sandra, I didn't understand her agenda, and I could always come back to her. So I was just about to say thanks and escape to the fresh air, when she started up again.

'How old are you, my dear?'

'Nearly thirty.'

'And you've worked since . . .?'

'Since I left school at eighteen.'

'How did you start? In the police?'

'No,' I said unexpansively.

'Do you work for a big company?'

She had my card. No point in lying. 'No.'

'So it's just you two?'

'Yes.'

'Aren't you brave!' she said. 'I was a career woman.'

'Oh. Early retirement?' I fished. I had no idea what she could have done. She wasn't stupid, at all. But neither was she a professional type – not a doctor or a lawyer or an accountant. Maybe a kindergarten teacher. And her manner had the all-embracing, cosy reassurance of an old-fashioned nurse. But no nurse or teacher ever earned enough to take early retirement in this kind of style.

'Not very early,' she said. 'I'd done my bit.'

Perhaps she'd been a hairdresser, or beautician. I could see her running a chain of shops. 'Were you in business?'

'Sort of,' she said. 'Are you married?'

'No,' I said. I must have spoken more sharply than I'd intended, because she stepped up the sympathy.

'Never mind,' she said. 'Mr Right will come along any day.'

'I'm sure,' I said, smiling blandly in my turn. I wasn't going to tell her that Mr Right probably had come along; the problem was that I was Ms Wrong.

'And you'll be wanting to get on the road, won't you. It's a long way to London.' She picked up my card from the table in front of her. 'And don't worry, Alex Tanner, I've got your number.'

Friday, 1 April

Chapter Fourteen

We stayed overnight in Doncaster at a cheapish chain hotel near the racecourse. I was too knackered to drive back to London.

Nick was delighted. She'd never stayed in a hotel as a paying guest before, though, when she could, she slipped in to big Paddington hotels to crash a night in an empty room. She enjoyed swaggering openly through the lobby, signing in and taking the key. She even enjoyed the almost inedible steak they produced in the hotel coffee-shop.

I was too tired to eat, and just sat watching her, sipping water and thinking about Jams. I didn't know what to tell her because I didn't know what was true. Luckily I didn't have to tell her anything until she got back tomorrow. Maybe I'd know more by then, though I couldn't see how.

A night's heavy, jet-lagged sleep didn't help. At breakfast, which I still wasn't able to eat, Nick said, 'What do we do now?'

'Go back to London.'

'Ring Maggie Whittaker before we go,' she said.

'What do you mean? I don't even have her phone number,' I said blankly. 'And what should I ring her for?'

Nick sighed with elaborate patience. 'The sooner you come back on line, the better. Since America you've been as thick as a brick.'

'Explain,' I said.

'First, I've got Maggie's number. It was on her telephone. Second, you don't know how much of Sandra Balmer to believe, right?'

'Right!'

'You thought Jacob was dead soon after he left the hotel, right?'

'Right!'

'And if only Sandra says he's alive since, maybe she's lying, right?'

'Right!'

'When we saw Maggie Whittaker, she said something you didn't pick up. She said she hadn't seen Jacob *to talk to* since his mother's funeral.'

My brain kicked in. 'You're right, she did.'

'And I didn't say anything because you always tell me to shut up and let you handle it,' said Nick smugly.

'I've never told you to shut up in public,' I said.

'You would if I ever spoke,' she said.

'Mrs Whittaker? Maggie? Alex Tanner here.'

Excited greetings. Could she help?

'I hope so. You said you hadn't seen Jacob "to talk to" since the funeral, last September.'

'I did.'

'But have you seen him and not talked, since?'

'Aye. Once or twice, he's been in and out of the house.'

'When was that?'

'Mebbe six weeks later. End of October time, early November. I noticed because I thought he was in America, but there he was next door. I'd have spoken if he would – I smiled at him – but he made out not to see me, so I didn't push it. He always kept himself to himself.'

We went straight down the motorway with *no* stops, despite the lingering glances and hinting coughs Nick produced every time a Services sign flashed by.

I drove and thought. Nick was going through my Chicago notes on Jacob, again, and jotting down ideas of her own.

We were south of Northampton – nearly back to civilization – when she spoke.

'D'you want some input on this?'

Unusual tact, for her. 'Go ahead,' I said.

'Known haunts and associates,' she said.

'Done those. Waiting to talk to Abraham Master.'

She sighed. 'That's the Doncaster end. But he didn't go straight back to Doncaster, he stayed in London. Not just overnight. And although he was *seen* by Maggie Whittaker once or twice, he wasn't *living* at that house. So where was he?'

'At Sandra's?'

'Could be. But we don't believe Sandra much, and you didn't ask her for details, anyway.'

'She wouldn't have given them,' I said defensively.

'She might. Anyway, you could have asked.'

'OK, I could have asked. Get to the point.'

'The point is that for three years before he went to Chicago he was working for a merchant bank. He must have lived somewhere. He must have *known* people, even if he didn't like them. It's an angle, anyway. Want me to suss it out?'

'How?'

'Start with Grace, get her to find the bank. His college must know. They give you references, Mary keeps telling me that, that's why I had to be nice to my teachers at college so the medical schools would take me. His references'll be on file there: Grace can get us the info. Then we go to the bank, follow it up. Colleagues, addresses and all that.'

When I got back to London the first thing I had to do was see Eddy. Nick might as well get straight to work on an angle I certainly should have thought of myself. I wasn't pleased, but Jams wasn't paying me to keep a good self-image.

'OK, go for it,' I said.

'Mind if I talk the case over with Grace? What we know, what we need to know?'

I wasn't mad on that either, but it could be useful.

'OK,' I said. 'Just don't tell Grace the details Jams told me about having sex with Jacob.'

'Why?'

'Jams wouldn't like it. Confidential.'

Nick shrugged. 'If you say so.'

'I do.'

Eddy'd already bought my drink when I got there. The Churchill is a cavernous, ugly pub, my local. It was nearly empty and it smelt of stale beer and cigarette smoke. It always did. I didn't usually mind. I was in a lousy temper I realized, as I sat down opposite him. 'I got you a lager and lime,' he said, pushing it across to me.

That's what I usually drink, when it's warm. It was warm today, but I didn't want it.

I made an effort, took the glass and thanked him. He looked like himself. Broad, beefy, wedged into a loud check suit, with a red face and twinkling piggy eyes. 'So how's my sexy Alex?' he said.

'I'm not sexy and I'm not yours,' I said, grumpy despite myself.

'Give me the chance and I'll put that right,' he said.

'Lay off, Eddy.'

'Pardon me for living.'

'Sorry and all that. I'm a bit edgy today.'

'Got your period, have you?'

Deep breath. Smile. 'How's your prostate, Eddy?'

'All the better for seeing you.'

I couldn't dent him. Get on with it. 'Why are we here?'

'I always like to see you, princess.'

'Me too. But you're a busy man. So, why wouldn't you talk about my dad over the phone? Do you know who he is?'

'Not exactly know. D'you want a bit of background?'

I didn't. Since starting on the track of my father I'd felt solid ground turn into a trapdoor, leaving me dangling over darkness. But I'd made a deal with Barty, so I gritted my teeth and nodded.

'A while back when you were just a nipper I was worried about your ma. When she first wasn't herself.'

'When she went off her head, you mean.'

'Come off it, Alex. You don't have to be tough with your uncle Eddy. It can't've been easy for you, any of it.'

'I coped,' I said brusquely.

'Yeah, you did later, all credit to you. But I was worried. You were only four then, and the wankers from the Social were taking you into care, and I reckoned then that if you had a dad, he might look after you. So I asked your ma, us two being close and all.'

'I expect you were feeling guilty because you were dicking her.'

'Maybe I was, maybe I wasn't. I don't reckon you've the right to call me on it, either way. And I won't let you talk about your ma like that. She deserves some respect. Got it?'

He folded his short, thick arms across his massive chest and glared at me. It was an intimidating, threatening glare. I'd never seen it before, but I could imagine it in an interrogation room just before he assisted a suspect to the floor.

I dropped my eyes. 'Got it,' I said, and the ground seemed more solid under my feet, though I'd die before I let him know it.

'So your ma told me a bit about herself and him. And she made me promise not to tell anyone.'

'She didn't mean me.'

'She said, anyone.'

'She's told me a bit already. I know he was a taxi-driver she met in a pub.'

Eddy took a long pull at his Newcastle Brown and smacked his lips. 'She told you that?'

'Yes.'

'Bit of a porky,' he said. 'To spare your feelings, I reckon.'

'To *spare* my feelings?'

'Yeah. Nobody likes not being wanted, it stands to reason.'

'Who wasn't wanted? What are you talking about, Eddy?'

'So what we're doing now, we're going over to discuss it with your mother.'

I laughed. 'That's stupid, Eddy. You can't *discuss* anything with her. She's got Alzheimer's, you know that.'

'But some days she's better than others. *You* know *that*. Three weeks back, when Carol and I visited, she knew us. Only for a few minutes, I grant you, but she knew us all right.'

Eddy and his wife visited Mum every month. More than I did, maybe. That made me feel guilty too.

I drank my lager and lime.

Eddy patted my hand. 'Listen, love, you're a brave one and a good one but you're not thinking straight about this. Why didn't you ask your mother yourself?'

'Because – because she's out of it.'

'You don't want to go behind her back. It's not the right thing. Come on, let's give it a go.'

'I'll see her by myself,' I said, and pushed my glass away. 'I hate lager and lime.'

'Me too,' he said. 'It's a whore's drink, same as port and lemon. I'm going to come with you, princess. Trust your uncle Eddy. You've just got your under-wear in an uproar because it's your time of the month.'

'Eddy, watch my lips. I do *not* have my period,' I said.

'Good. You'll let me come with you, then.'

Chapter Fifteen

It's a twenty-minute drive from the semi-posh, semi-rough street near Notting Hill where I live to the red-brick Victorian hospital off the North Circular Road where my mother waits to die.

When we got there, Eddy took charge. He spoke to the nurses and led the way to the grubby day-room. While we sat waiting for my mother he fished a pound bar of Cadbury's nut milk chocolate out of his pocket and gave it to me. 'She'll like her choccy, anyway,' he said. 'Chin up, princess.'

Five long minutes later my mother shuffled in. She used to be pretty. Now, though she's only in her forties, she looks old. Her hair, once light brown, is faded and dull. It's shoulder-length, parted in the middle. It clings to her head in sweaty clumps, because the nurses don't wash it enough, and when they do they don't bother to rinse out the shampoo. I could do what some of the other patients' relatives do, come in and help look after her, wash her hair and rinse it properly. I could, but I'm not going to, and I'm not usually guilty about it.

She was wearing a knee-length grey wool skirt,

overwashed and shrunk and bobbled, and a green blouse, too big. I recognized the cardigan: I'd bought it for her last Christmas. It had been a light clear pink, because she liked (likes?) pastels. Now it was sludgy pinko-grey, from the hospital laundry.

She has a facial twitch, possibly from the drugs they give her for schizophrenia, possibly from the Alzheimer's. Her shuffle might be from either as well. Her eyes are usually dull, and today they went over Eddy and me without recognition or understanding. She turned to the nurse who'd brought her – a fifty-year-old Jamaican built like the Albert Memorial – in what looked like panic and clutched her arm. 'That's all right, my dear, that's all right,' said the nurse, pushing her away and into the room.

I went up, hugged my mother and showed her the chocolate. She followed the chocolate to a chair next to me, and I began to feed it to her, piece by piece.

I talk to her as if she can understand. I've always feared that she might be making more sense inside than ever comes out. 'I've just come back from Chicago,' I said. 'I was doing some research on a documentary about legalizing drugs.'

She mumbled something. She'd tried to cram in more than she could chew and chocolate was oozing out from the corners of her mouth and trickling down her face. I took a Kleenex and leant forward to wipe it for her, still talking. 'There's more money about,' I said. 'I think the recession is almost over. And my private detective work is building up all the time.'

She was still mumbling, and now I could hear it. 'Chicago Chicago,' she was saying.

'That's right, Chicago,' I said.

'Frank,' she said.

'Frank?'

She spat out the rest of the chocolate. 'Stupid stupid stupid,' she snarled.

She'd made a mess on the carpet. It wasn't a clean carpet. In a State-provided underfunded long-stay mental hospital, what did you expect? I mopped the mess anyway.

Eddy was making an extraordinary noise, like a bull in torment. Then I realized he was singing. 'Chicago, Chicago, that toddlin' town. Chicago, Chicago, I'll show you around.'

My mother smiled. 'Yes yes yes,' she said. 'Yes.' She took the tissues from my hand and began sucking the chocolate mess off them. I let her. She seemed to be enjoying it, and her enjoyment is rare and fragile.

Eddy didn't mind: he was well into the song. 'Bet your bottom dollar you lose the blues . . .'

My mother joined in – 'In Chicago, Chicago, my home town!'

Her voice was better than Eddy's. High, sweet and on the note.

'Hello, Sukie. You like Frank Sinatra, don't you?' said Eddy.

'Yes,' said my mother. 'Hello, Eddy, how's Carol?'

'She's fine. She sends her love.' Eddy stood up and took my mother's sticky hands in his beefy paws. 'Me and Alex have come to talk to you about something important, Sukie.'

'I forget,' she said, panicking.

Eddy's voice boomed again. 'The cigarette that bears the lipstick traces – the airline ticket to romantic places . . .'

My mother joined in and I had to endure two verses and a chorus before Eddy judged she'd calmed down. Still holding her hands, he said, 'Alex wants to know about her dad.'

'She's too young,' my mother said. 'She's too young, Eddy. Only a kid.'

'This is Alex,' said Eddy, gently for him. 'She's a big girl now.'

My mother turned to me, confused. 'Pleased to meet you,' she said.

'It's hopeless, Eddy,' I said, hurt by not being recognized. Stupidly hurt, because sometimes she knows me, and anyhow for her probably the less she knows about anything the better.

'Shut it, princess,' he said. 'I'm handling this. Listen to me, Susan love, Alex is well grown up now.'

'Is she? Where is she? Who took care of her?'

'You did, love,' said Eddy. 'Most of the time. Alex is fine, she's all grown up and happy. I think I should tell her what you told me.'

'Do you?' My mother was crying now. I gave her another piece of chocolate and she stuffed it in her mouth.

'I'm going to tell her,' said Eddy. 'It's the right thing.'

'Are you sure?' More chocolate. Gobble gobble.

'Trust me, Sukie.'

'If you say so, Eddy!' I wiped her dribbling mouth. 'Can we sing again?' she said. 'Can we sing "My Way", Eddy?'

Back in the car, I said, 'I hate "My Way".'

'Me too,' said Eddy. 'Look how much we've got in common, Alex. We both hate lager and lime and "My Way". Is this the beginning of a beautiful relationship?'

'In your dreams, and get your sweaty hand off my knee,' I said impatiently. 'Do you *ever* stop chasing tail, Eddy?'

'Not since I was fourteen,' he said smugly. 'And most of the time I catch it. Can you drive and listen at the same time?'

'Yes.'

'Then I'll tell you what I know about your dad.'

Chapter Sixteen

I sat alone in the Churchill drinking straight lager, looked at the piece of paper Eddy had given me, and thought over what he'd told me.

I didn't know what he'd been making such a fuss about. My mother's story was a very simple one. Very sad too, but then she'd always, to me, been a very sad woman.

Her parents – still alive, as far as Eddy knew, but he'd last seen them twenty-six years ago – lived in Ealing, a suburb about two miles west of Notting Hill. Her father had been a clerk in the Town Hall then. Her mother was a housewife.

They were also called Tanner. She hadn't changed her name. John and Maureen Tanner. My grand-parents. I tried it on my tongue – 'Grandpa John' – 'Granny Maureen' – and laughed. The group at the next table, Irish labourers at a very late lunch break, didn't even look round. The patrons of the Churchill often talked to themselves.

My mother had been a normal child, gone to the local Catholic secondary school and been above aver-age academically. That surprised me: unfairly, because come to think of it she'd never been thick, just mentally ill. Then when she was sixteen, she'd got pregnant. By an ultra-Catholic, ultra-married master at her school. He'd blamed her, saying she'd tempted him. My grandparents (who I hadn't bonded with, at the start, but who I liked less and less the more I thought about it) had also blamed her, and insisted that the baby (me) be given up for adoption. She'd refused, and run away. A Catholic society for unmarried mothers had taken her in until two months after I was born, then found her a council flat in the high-rise block in Fulham where we'd lived, some of the time, when I was growing up.

Her parents had refused to see her while she kept the baby. My father (Eddy didn't know his name) had also refused to see me or have anything to do with me.

I thought about that. How did it make me feel?

Nothing. Absolutely nothing. Not rejected, or deserted, or belittled, although a counsellor would probably have said I was in denial. He'd never known me, after all. The person he'd rejected wasn't me. What he'd rejected were his responsibilities, and normal human feeling, because for a teacher to blame a sixteen-year-old pupil was absurd, and especially a gentle one like my mother.

If the story was true. It fitted with what I knew of my mother. She'd have been an attractive girl: slim, bright-eyed, pretty, responsive, loving. And naïve. A born victim. The men she'd lived with while I was growing up had all ripped her off, one way or another. No surprise that it had started early.

I folded up the piece of paper with my grandparents' name and address. The next step would be to see them, ask about the family, get them to identify my father, if they were still alive, and pay him a visit, if he was still alive. No big emotional scenes: just checking the bloodline for hereditary illnesses.

Then I'd have to give my answer to Barty. But not yet.

Back in my empty flat (Nick must still have been over at Grace Macarthy's) I took off my DMs and lay down on the sofa for a quick kip before I went out to Heathrow to meet Polly's flight.

I woke four hours later, in the chilly dusk. I'd well and truly overslept. I washed my face, brushed my teeth, and went downstairs to see if she'd arrived.

She had.

'Alex, Alex, Alex, oh my God! Isn't this wonderful, kiss kiss kiss, come on in, I went up to your flat and you were asleep so I didn't wake you because you must still be jet-lagged, it's much worse west to east, and I'm not tired because I've slept for ages and you're looking terrific and now we'll have fun. I can't believe it's actually you, it's not at all the same on the phone, Barty met me, gosh isn't he nice, you are lucky, and he's taking us somewhere great for dinner and it's booked and all fixed up, and now you must help me decide what to wear and see what you've got and I can lend you something if you like, oh, Alex, I'm so glad to see you. I could *burst*!'

'Barty met you?'

'Yes, didn't you ask him to?'

'I meant to meet you myself. I overslept.'

'He'll tell you about it at dinner, I expect . . .'

'What time are we having dinner?'

'He's picking us up at eight, so we've got an hour and a half to get ready.'

I looked round her living-room. It had started out tidy – I'd cleaned it ready for her before I went to America – but now every piece of furniture was covered with clothes. As far as I knew she was only staying three days but it looked as if she'd brought the complete wardrobe for the female lead in a contemporary feature film, and to her own flat, which had plenty of her clothes in it already.

I cleared a chair by dumping its contents onto the floor, and sat down.

'I've so much to tell you, so much, oh I must do something with my face I look ancient, it's something to do with the time-zones and Einstein, it must be, I've left myself behind in Hong Kong and this is me a hundred years on . . .'

I stopped listening, and watched her. She didn't look old, of course. She looked like a beautiful giraffe. She always does. She's tall and thin with a small, large-eyed, appealing face and a long neck. She has dark hair, dark eyes, a short torso and endless slender legs. She had the central heating full on and was only wearing a teeshirt, a tiny pair of high-cut knickers and a silver ankle-chain.

When I spotted the ankle-chain my heart sank. They weren't currently fashionable, as far as I knew, so it must have been a present. From a man.

I pointed to the ankle-chain. 'Are they in again?'

She blushed. 'Not specially – not exactly – it was a present.'

I sighed. 'Don't tell me. From a bald, fat, selfish, dull, married man.'

'He's got plenty of hair,' she said defensively.

'On his head?'

'Some of it's on his head.'

'You've done it again, haven't you?'

She sat down next to me and hugged me impulsively. That's what the script would have said, *Polly sits down next to Alex and hugs her impulsively.* It wasn't so impulsive that it wasn't studied and graceful, but it wasn't dishonest either. It made me feel clumsy. I tried to hug her back and our arms got tangled, so I pulled away and said, 'What is it?'

'Alex, I need to talk to you. We must talk.'

'We would be talking if you weren't talking about talking. Get on with it, Polly. Cut to the chase.'

'I think I'm going to marry him.'

An hour later I knew all about Polly's man. He was thirty-five, a top international banker, tall and handsome and kind and stinking rich. He was fit because he worked out (but not obsessively) he played squash (very well) he was considerate with subordinates and ruthless in business and although he was busy busy busy, he still had time for a full social life. He drank (but not too much), he didn't smoke (but he didn't mind smokers), he didn't use drugs, he had a great sense of humour, and although he'd never been married (he was waiting for the right woman, the right time) he'd had successful long-standing love affairs and he was still friends with his ex-lovers. He had a flat in London and, when they were married he wanted Polly to choose a house in Gloucestershire. And a dog.

When she'd started telling me about it, I'd settled comfortably on her sofa and prepared for the cruel and unusual punishment of being babbled at by women in love, twice in one week.

It didn't take me very long to spot that it wasn't the same experience at all. Jams had been describing a man she loved. Polly was describing an acquaintance.

An acquaintance she might marry, true. She was listing his advantages as a husband. Jams hadn't been, and not just, I didn't think, because her precious Jacob wasn't as much of a catch as Polly's Magnus.

If Polly's Magnus was as she described, there had to be something fundamentally wrong with him because no personality came through at all. Only a collection of attributes and habits.

Halfway through I tried to stop her. 'Do you love him?' I said. 'Do you actually want to spend the rest of your life with him?'

I was trying to measure myself on their scale of feeling, and I thought I'd come somewhere between Polly and Jams. I wouldn't, if I talked about Barty, gush like Jams, but that would partly be because gushing wasn't my way. Nor would I get as involved as Polly had in the practical details of how to assess the man. I'd be thinking about assessing my feelings for the man.

That wasn't what Polly was talking about. She wanted me to judge him. Was he right for her? Not, did she think he was right for her?

'Polly, he sounds ideal. He sounds too ideal to be true. He sounds like a rising-thirty's fantasy.'

'What's with you?' said Polly. 'You've always been on at me to pick better men.'

That was hard to answer, because it was partly true. 'I wanted them not to be married,' I said.

'But you complained about them being unsuccessful. And bald. And not very attractive.'

I had. But that was because I thought she'd buried her life in them, and done it on purpose. I'd thought she'd been bailing herself out in buckets, and throwing it away. I'd thought there'd been no emotional sense in the relationships.

It was too much to tackle now. So I set my face to lively interest and Polly diverted herself to what we were going to wear when we went out. That always engaged her. On her deathbed she'd be planning the most suitable outfit for a deathbed.

*

Just before eight I popped upstairs to my flat to change. Now fully awake, I noticed the notes by the telephone. While I'd been sleeping on the sofa, Nick and Barty between them had been tramping in and out and running my life.

Nick's note:

1. Have seen Grace, staying with her tonight. Working on Jacob, will report to you here 11am Sat unless you cancel.
2. Have typed and printed your Chicago drugs doc notes. On printer.
3. Alan Protheroe rang again. Said all done, you'd call Sat.
4. Carl Nabokov rang, will ring again. Have put his London hostel phone number in address book.
5. Barty came by, wanted you to sleep on, said he'd fetch Polly and see you both for dinner, pick-up 8pm (didn't know if you'd want this, didn't argue).

Barty's note:

Forgive interference as per Nick's note. You looked peaceful, asleep, didn't want to wake you. Dinner on me.

As I changed (no hard decisions here: I only had two expensive-restaurants outfits, which I'd worn for Barty so often already that he might very well propose to them) I wondered why I wasn't annoyed. I hate interference, at least I thought I did. Maybe I didn't hate competent, useful interference. Maybe if it was competent and useful I should reclassify it as help and welcome it. Maybe when Nick went to medical school and the position with Barty was resolved one way or another I could confiscate their sets of keys to my flat and get back to intelligent life, Jim, as we know it.

Saturday, 2 April

Chapter Seventeen

Good restaurant, good food, good wine, good conversation, and bloody good to be home, I thought when
Barty'd dropped us back and I'd closed the bedroom
door on an exhausted Polly.

It was just after midnight. I went upstairs to my
flat, hung up my smart clothes, showered, put on old
grey leggings and an outsize grey sweatshirt, rolled up
my sleeves, put some Liszt (my latest craze) on the
CD player and got down to work.

I unpacked my Chicago luggage, sorted the dirty
clothes and put the first load in to wash. Then I
checked through Nick's version of my notes for Alan,
made one or two amendments, and put them in a
large envelope with the Polaroid snaps of suggested
locations.

That was Alan done. Now for Jams. I moved into
the kitchen with all the notes I'd made in Chicago and
the tapes of the interviews with Maggie Whittaker
and Sandra Balmer. Time to get the action board
sorted.

*

An hour, two cups of coffee and a CD later, I stepped back and looked at the cork board next to my kitchen window which now displayed the results of my trawl through everything I'd done since Sunday.

Top left, the graduation photograph of Jacob. Nick was right, I had been slow and stupid yesterday. I should have checked with Maggie Whittaker that the woman in the photograph really was Jacob's mother, as I supposed. I could check it with Abraham Master on Monday.

My action list now read:

> *see Abraham Master re sightings of Jacob, any other info (?foto, ?Tubbies' finances)*
> *?Chicago for Eng Lit*
> *?the loop*
> *Sandra Balmer true/false? motive if lying?*
> *merchant bank stuff – Nick*
> *my grandparents: telephone number still extant?*

It was now getting on for two in the morning. There was only one thing on the list I could do anything about then, so I went next door and rang directory enquiries. Yes, there was a number for John Tanner in Ealing, the same number Eddy had given me. So my grandfather had been alive enough to pay his last telephone bill.

I still wasn't sleepy. I abandoned Liszt and Schubert, took the washing out, hung it up, put another load in, then sat down to go through what was left of my mail after Nick had sifted it.

Mostly junk, which I tore and chucked mechanically, wondering if anyone ever actually bought the strange things companies wrote to me about, and if anyone believed that they would really win a million pounds if they ordered a pair of walking-boots with built-in torch *within seven days*!

Then I stopped, dead. Junk mail. Mail. Jacob had left Carl's apartment as his forwarding address from International House, but I'd gone through Jacob's things, and there hadn't been any letters. None at all. And Jams had written to Jacob, several times. Even if Jacob was the only person in the Western world not to be on *someone's* junk mail list after living in the same place for a year, Jams' letters should have been there.

I added *Ring Carl – ?letters* to my list, and went to bed.

I never go shopping with people. I dislike the process, and if it has to be done, then I see no reason why more than one person should suffer.

But Polly woke very early on Saturday, she wanted to be with me, and she wanted to shop, and there was no way, at eight o'clock in the morning, that I could muster up the energy to resist her. Not delicately enough to leave our friendship intact.

So I rang Nick to tell her not to come round till one or later, and by nine o'clock Polly and I were in Knightsbridge.

If I was Polly, I'd find choosing clothes very hard.

One, she has scads of money which she's prepared to spend on them, while I look at a grossly overpriced jacket and see it in terms of so many more units of my pension plan. Two, nearly everything she tries on looks great, whereas I have to dress to counteract my flaws, and most things make me look squat or hippy or top-heavy.

Polly was like an assembly-line quality checker. Try, try, try, no. Try, yes. Try, try, no. She'd ask for my advice ('That's the fun of a shopping trip!') and she'd dismiss it ('Oh Alex, not a *neutral colour*. *Not* this season.').

I like other people's skills. This was hers. I didn't rate the outcome – she'd look gorgeous in a sack – but I marvelled at the process. It was like watching Barty edit a documentary.

We'd done Walton Street. We'd done Harrods and Harvey Nichols. Polly was the shopper, I was the pack horse, and when we arrived in Bond Street, I'd marvelled enough. I went on strike.

'Coffee,' I said.

'It's only an hour till you have to get back. We haven't even looked at Farhi or Ozbek. And I have a sentimental attachment to Fenwicks.'

'You can do them without me.'

'It's no fun alone,' she wailed.

'In here,' I said, and shouldered open the glittering doors to a glittering café, with marble floors and marble tables and brightly polished brass fittings. I found an empty table, entrenched myself behind the carrier-bags, and wriggled my toes in my boots.

Polly fetched two cups of coffee from a counter which offered a choice of eighty-two varieties, some of them decaffeinated, most of them flavoured with something else. There were little cards on the table telling us that Sophie, the proprietor of the shop, had dedicated her life to our coffee enjoyment. Either she was lying or she needed psychiatric help. Or maybe it was a US franchise.

My coffee enjoyment was gulping it down, and I did. It tasted all right, but hardly a life's work, and why on earth would you mess up decent coffee with vanilla?

Polly sipped abstractedly, and I could see confidences were coming on. 'I'm afraid of being lonely,' she said. 'That's the truth of it. Do you think that's a reason to get married?'

What I thought was that one female friend-thing was enough for a morning. Shopping, OK. Heart to heart, OK. Both? Not if I could avoid it.

I re-arranged the carrier bags abstractedly.

'Alex?' said Polly. 'I know you heard me. Say something.'

'I think you can be lonelier forced to be close to people you don't want to be close to than by yourself,' I said. 'I was always lonely with my foster-parents. Marriage could be like that.'

'I was very lonely in Hong Kong, at first.'

'Stands to reason.'

'It wasn't just the different place, it was having no future. No future that I knew I wanted . . . That could be why I took up with Magnus. That's what Richard said. He's my boss, very sweet. But I don't know. Put your mind to it, Alex. I trust your judgement about people. You were right about Clive.'

That was no recommendation. Anyone would have been right about Clive, Polly's last, useless man. A random poll of the nearest kindergarten would have rated him a no-hoper on day one. But Polly was steam-rollering on. 'I want you to meet Magnus, and tell me what you think.'

'When?' I said guardedly.

'He's going to be in London. This weekend. And I wondered – Alex – would you have dinner with us tonight? You and Barty? Magnus would pay, and you could both give me your opinion.'

'Barty may not be free.'

'He is. I asked him on the way from Heathrow and he said it was fine with him but I had to ask you, it was your decision.'

'Where's Magnus staying?' I said, fearing he'd be downstairs in her flat, which could so easily lead to him being upstairs in mine.

'At his flat,' she said. 'I told you, he has a flat in London.

'So you did . . . Why does it matter what I think of your man?'

Polly looked at me. She was getting intense. She'd be crying, any minute. 'You're my friend, Alex. I don't want to lose you. I trust you.

'You won't lose me,' I said. 'Even if Magnus and I hate each other's guts, it won't make any difference to you and me, Polly. Especially as it sounds as if

Magnus spends his whole time somewhere else. If you get a dog, now – that's a different matter. I'll come with you to choose the dog, because I'll be seeing a darn sight more of him. And so will you. Get your priorities straight, girl.'

'I'm serious,' said Polly.

'You've plenty of other friends,' I said, trying to push her away a little. I'm not good with sentimentality.

'Yes, but you can lose them when you pair up . . . That's why I'm so pleased about Barty.'

'What do you mean?' I said warily. 'Get me another cup of coffee, will you? And hold the vanilla flavour, this time.'

'They have eighty-two varieties. Live a little.'

'I do. I live and I drink coffee. I don't live *through* the coffee.'

So she fetched me another cup, but it didn't distract her. 'I'm pleased about Barty because you and he are obviously a permanent fixture, and he and I get on so well, so when the children come and you'll have to look after them and I visit, then he won't mind if I'm in the house when he gets home, and he won't make those faces like, get your awful friend out of here, can't I have a drink in peace?'

'You're taking too much for granted,' I said.

'Rubbish. You love him. He loves you. And he's got money. And he's kind. It's so rare to find the one person, Alex, you wouldn't pass it up. Like poor Jams, she was absolutely sure she'd found him, and then something happens—'

'We don't know that something happened to Jacob. Jams may just have blown a quickie out of all proportion.'

'But that isn't what you really believe.'

'I really believe there's no such thing as perfect love. But that may only be because I've spent hours shopping and I'm grumpy. Come on, let's hit Farhi.'

Chapter Eighteen

It was just after one when I reached the flat. Polly was still safely in Bond Street, there was no sign of Nick but there were two messages on the answering machine. Carl Nabokov wanted me to return his call. Nick would be by about two o'clock.

Good. An hour. I'd spend it on a run. I hadn't had any proper exercise for nearly a week and I could feel my arteries clogging and cellulite colonising my thighs.

Three miles later, bathed in virtuous sweat and with aching shins, I collapsed onto the sofa. Nick was waiting for me, excited. 'Alex— hey, Alex—'

'Water,' I said.

'This is important!'

'Water. And towel. This minute.'

She fetched them. 'Now will you listen?

'Yes,' I said, gulping the water. A week without running had been too long.

'It's about the Tubbies. Grace rang a man in Aberdeen who knows all about sects, and he told her about them. They're very peculiar and they disapprove of nearly everything, which we sort of knew, but we didn't know one crucial thing. They don't approve of bodies, except for fighting righteous wars. They're very into fighting. But they don't have sex. At all. So they never have children, not of their own. They adopt, or they did, but then when abortion and single mothers took over they couldn't find anyone to adopt, I suppose, so Jacob's probably one of the last of the English Tubbies, age-wise.'

'No he isn't. There were children at the service.'

'Anyway, he's got real parents, somewhere, or a mother at least, and he'll know who she is because they're always told that they've been saved and who from. The more sin the child inherits, the better, apparently. Tubmaster always took prostitutes' children, when he could. So I'd have been a candidate, except Mum didn't know about the Tubbies, plus I was dead useful because I took her to the top of the council housing list. But do you see, Alex? He must have known. And he may have gone looking for his family. And there's a mother out there who might not have wanted Jacob to pop up again.'

'Jacob might not have wanted to pop up again either,' I said. 'But all the same – it's an angle. It's definitely an angle.'

'Master might know where he came from. We can ask him. And Sandra Balmer might know.'

'Well done, Nick,' I said.

She just nodded. 'I've put my notes on the Tubbies in the Jacob file. Plus I've got the name of the merchant bank. On the action board. They'll be closed for the Easter weekend, I suppose, or maybe not Grace says because of the foreign stock markets being open.'

'D'you want to try them?'

'No,' she said, and blushed. 'I'm going away with Grace. To her cottage. Until Monday night. Leaving now. If that's OK with you?'

'Sure,' I said. 'Thanks. My best to Grace.'

I didn't smile with relief until the door had closed behind her. Then I took off my clothes, put a piano concerto of Liszt's on the CD, loudly, and went upstairs to shower.

One less person to deal with. Now if Magnus had missed his plane and Barty could be persuaded to take Polly out to dinner without me, I could have an evening to myself. But at least I was more or less guaranteed an afternoon, I gloated as I dressed. Clean jeans. Clean sweatshirt, short-sleeves, navy blue, no logo. Bare sore feet.

Back in the kitchen heading for coffee, I realised I was hungry. I had some tea-cakes that needed eating in the freezer compartment of the fridge. Twenty-four of them. I'd bought a jumbo-sized packet of forty-eight, reduced at Tesco. It was taking me a while to get through them: I don't much like tea-cakes and the defrosting was too much hassle. Generally, when I'm hungry, I eat right then. I'd tried toasting them, frozen, but they'd set fire to the toaster.

I took out three, sliced them thin, shoved them in the toaster and watched them carefully. They didn't burn, and with jam, they didn't taste too bad. And they were cheap.

Then I poured a second cup of coffee and sat down at the kitchen table for an orgy of telephoning.

Carl Nabokov first. The hostel office put me through to his room. No answer. I left a have-rung-back, please-ring-back message.

I rang Alan Protheroe next, gave him ten minutes of reassurance and logged the call as twelve, for expenses.

Then I tried Jams and left a please-ring message on her answering machine. She should have been back by now; she was probably asleep.

Fourth time lucky with Maggie Whittaker. 'This is Alex Tanner . . . Hi. No, I'm in London. There's one or two things I'd like to ask you. Is this a bad time? . . . Great. Could you describe Janet Stone to me?'

I looked at Jacob's graduation photograph on the action board as she talked. That was the woman, all right. I crossed ?*foto* off my list.

'Brilliant, thanks. Now, Janet wasn't his biological mother, was she?'

Maggie laughed, a hearty studio-audience bellow, and I held the receiver away from my ear. 'No chance, me love. Them being Tubbies. They don't hold with the flesh. It wouldn't do me, I can tell you, but they never do no harm to anyone, more than you can say for most of us.'

'Who was Jacob's real mother?'

'I dunno, me duck. Ask Sandra.'

'Why? I didn't think she and Janet saw each other after Janet's marriage.'

'They did until the baby arrived. Sandra made the arrangements, but it wasn't hers, I know that.'

'Thanks, I'll talk to her about it . . . Next thing – does "the loop" mean anything to you?'

Baffled burble from distant Armthorpe.

'Never mind,' I said. 'Jacob mentioned it to his girlfriend, he said "the real him was in the loop". I thought it might be a place round you, or a Yorkshire expression . . . No?'

'Not that I've ever heard, me duck.'

'Last thing. Tell me about Sandra.'

'What do you want to know?'

'Anything. What's she like? Who are her friends? What did she work at? I saw her last night and she was quite helpful, but I don't know what to make of her.'

I made notes while Maggie talked, and when she'd repeated herself three times, I thanked her and rang off.

Then I looked at my notes. *Bossy. Full of herself. Own business in London. Balmer Leisure Services.*

You never know. I fetched the telephone directories and started looking. I found Balmer Leisure Services in London, North West, an address in Queen's Park. About a mile north-east of me.

I scribbled the address on a piece of paper, stuck it on the board. Maybe later I'd snoop, although on a holiday weekend the chances were it would be closed. Whatever it was, it sounded shady.

While I was at it I added *?Tubbies' children* to my action list. Then the phone rang, inches away, and made me jump.

'Alex? Carl.'

'Hi, Carl.'

'Great to hear your voice,' he said.

Uh-oh. 'Just business,' I said.

'Business?' he said.

He sounded so let down that I repented and warmed up my tone to friendly/playful. 'Jacob's my case, remember?'

'But it's a holiday weekend. The British Library's closed Monday, and I thought maybe we could spend the day together. How about it?'

No way. But I didn't want to offend him either because I wanted his co-operation. 'I'm very busy,' I said, 'but I'd like to see you . . . Can I come back to you on it?'

'Would you like to see me? Really?'

His 'really' was a charming, furry American sound. I remembered his skin and his wonderful eyes and his body between my legs and felt my grip slipping. 'Really,' I said. 'I'll be back to you. But I have a question. Your apartment was Jacob's forwarding address, right?'

'Right.'

'Was there no mail forwarded at all?'

Pause. 'No,' he said.

'Not even any letters from Jams?'

'Nothing,' he said. 'Otherwise I'd have given them to you . . . When will you be back to me? About Monday?'

'Tomorrow morning,' I said.

It took me a while to disentangle myself. When I put the phone down, I sat and thought.

The letters worried me. It was *possible* that International House had done no forwarding. It was *possible* that the US mail had malfunctioned. But it wasn't likely.

Either Carl was lying, or Jams was.

I didn't want it to be Carl, because if it was, then I'd have to see him again, and I didn't want to.

Back to the phone. I dialled Jams' number and talked through the answering machine. 'Jams? Are you there? This is Alex. Pick up, please, pick up.'

No response. I left it a minute, then dialled again. 'Pick up. I need to speak to you. Pick up.'

This time, a sleepy voice. 'Alex? Alex?'

'Hi . . . No news, I'm afraid. But something I want to ask you. You said Jacob had told you he came from "an ordinary home". Is that true?'

Pause. Then: 'No. He told me about his faith.'

'So why didn't you tell me?'

'Because I knew what you'd think. I'm a believing Christian too, and I know what people think of us, now. They think we're peculiar.'

'Not necessarily,' I said.

'Are you a Christian?' she said hopefully.

'No,' I said.

'What are you?'

'I don't know. But the point is, you kept information back from me. When I drew a blank in Chicago and I only had the hotel address in London, you could have told me then about the Tubbies.'

'The Tubbies?'

'Jacob's church up north. Christ's Children of the Fountain of the Water of Life. They were an obvious contact point.'

'Sorry, Alex.'

'Did you lie to me about anything else?'

'No.'

'You wrote to Jacob at International House?'

'Of course.'

'How many times?'

'Five,' she said.

'Why didn't you write to him in England c/o the Tubbies?'

'Because of what he said.'

'What did he say?'

'He said I could write to him in Chicago but on no account to try and get in touch with him in England. He said it might be dangerous and that I should wait to hear from him.'

'He said it might be dangerous? And you didn't tell me?'

Pause. 'Sorry, Alex.'

'Did he say why?'

'No. He said he didn't know what he might be getting into, and he wasn't sure, but there was an outside chance it might be dangerous.'

'And you didn't tell me?'

Pause. 'No, I didn't.'

'Why?'

'I'm not sure. He only said, an outside chance.

And it was months ago. And I'd almost begun to wonder . . .'

'What?'

'If maybe he'd said that to put me off. If maybe . . .'

Pause. 'Maybe he was planning to ditch you?'

'I've only thought that in the middle of the night,' she said defensively. 'Once or twice. All the rest of the time I knew he loved me. You must understand.'

'I understand,' I said, not too sympathetically, 'but I'm not over the moon about it. Is there anything else you should tell me? About "the loop", for instance?'

Long pause. 'No. No, there really isn't, I promise. Are you going to give up the case?'

Fat chance, when it was just warming up, but I wasn't going to let her get away scot-free. 'No, but I'll have to up my fees. For possible danger. And I've worked over the days you paid me for.'

'OK,' she said submissively. 'Send me the bill, or do you want me to come over with a cheque?'

'Not now.'

'So, what have you found out?'

I told her that I'd seen Maggie Whittaker, and that she'd filled me in on the Tubbies. I didn't tell her anything else. I promised to be in touch tomorrow, and rang off as soon as I could.

I was beginning to have serious doubts about Jams. She'd presented herself as Little Miss Integrity. Now her story was creaking and shifting like snow before an avalanche, and I didn't want the Mountain Rescue people turning out for me. Had she seen Jacob in London, been rejected, and killed him, to preserve her dream? She didn't look like a killer, but then they often don't.

Sandra Balmer was as shady as a redwood forest, but that might just be her nature. I couldn't make sense of her involvement.

Nor of Carl's. But Jams had written to International House, I believed that, and something had happened to those letters, and he should know. At least part of Monday would have to be spent with him. And I'd take some condoms along, just in case.

Chapter Nineteen

'Oh brilliant, now it's just us, though you know I love
Barty, and I'm sorry if you and he really wanted to go
to bed tonight but I so want to be with you, and you
two have all the time in the world together, and now
we can get the duvet and snuggle up on the sofa and
you can tell me what you think of Magnus and we can
watch *Casablanca*. Do you want to watch *Casablanca*?'
said Polly, opening a bottle of Australian red.

If I drank any more wine I'd pass out. 'Water,' I
said. 'Water, please. And a piece of bread. What time is
it?'

Polly scuttled down to her kitchen, calling to me
as she went. 'It's only just before midnight, not late for
you, Alex, please, you don't want to go to sleep yet.'
She reappeared with a bottle of Perrier, a glass and a
stick of French bread. 'What did you think of him? Tell
me, tell me everything, you must have had a good
time because you drank a lot, didn't you, more than
I've ever seen you drink in a restaurant, so you must
have been relaxed – he has that effect on people, he's
so easy to get on with because he's so charming,
people say they feel as if they've known him for

years, and he's such a generous host, and he knows such a lot about wine—'

'True,' I said, nibbling the bread, visualising branches of Alcoholics Anonymous springing up all over the world in Magnus's charming wake as he drove his guests to drink. I gulped a glass of water, then another, and the room stopped rotating, though the sofa was still heaving gently.

Polly sat down beside me and anchored the sofa. 'I know you'll be honest,' she said. 'Tell me what you think. Please?'

Difficult. Magnus was the kind of non-person my memory-banks reject. All façade: a polished nothing with empty eyes. I hoped I'd never have to have dinner with him again. 'He's extraordinary,' I said.

'Isn't he?' Polly was looking at me eagerly. 'Do you think Barty liked him?'

I drank some more water and made an effort. 'Polly, why don't you follow your heart?'

'That's what Richard says.'

'Who's Richard?'

'I've *told* you, he's my boss.'

So she had. Only this morning. I must be even drunker than I'd thought. I closed my eyes. Bad mistake: the sofa heaved. I opened them to find that *Casablanca* was flickering away on the TV screen and that Polly had fetched the duvet from her bedroom and settled it over us. 'It's nice to be alone, isn't it?' she said. 'Odd thing about Magnus, he's a terrific person but he's not actually fun. For instance, I can't relax like this with him.'

I had to get into the girlie spirit somehow. 'What's he like in bed?' I said.

'Guess,' she said.

'No idea,' I said, and I didn't snap, which should have earned me all kinds of credit.

'The thing is – it's not exactly – that's sort of changed, hasn't it?'

'What?'

'Relationships. Casual sex.'

'You mean you haven't bonked?' I said, gulping water.

'I wish you wouldn't use that word.'

Deep breath. Mistake. Shallow breath, more water. 'Polly. I'm blasted, OK? Have a heart. Do you mean you haven't made love?'

'No,' said Polly defensively. 'Not that he doesn't want to.'

'How do you know?'

'He told me. Of course he does, anyway, he wants to marry me, he loves me. And we've kissed, of course.'

'Is he a good kisser?' I said. I'd last asked that question of my then best friend the year I turned twelve, and it had sounded fairly juvenile even then.

'He's a great kisser.'

'Great how?'

'Considerate.'

'Considerate,' I said, and then I lost it. I started to giggle and couldn't stop.

She began by pokering up, then she hit me with a

cushion, then she giggled with me, till we sobbed to an exhausted halt.

'Considerate,' she said, and we started again. Finally, she gasped out. 'You hate him, don't you?'

'Not hate.'

'Don't like.'

'Don't know,' I said.

'Don't want to know,' she said.

'Not my type. Too perfect.'

Pause, while we watched Humphrey Bogart's raincoat turn in an Oscar-winning performance as Humphrey Bogart's raincoat.

Then she said, 'What's Barty like in bed?'

I began to giggle. 'Considerate,' I said.

She hit me again, with two cushions this time.

'OK. He's bloody good. Better than Carl.'

'Who's Carl?'

'A graduate student I met in Chicago.' She looked shocked. 'Can it, Polly, he's only a one-nighter.'

'But I thought you loved Barty.'

'I probably do,' I said impatiently.

'Does Barty know?'

'Don't think so. Haven't told him.'

'You're taking a big risk,' she said. 'Aren't you? Don't you think? What would Barty do if he knew?'

'No idea,' I said.

'That's the thing about Barty, isn't it, he's very closed in, just like you.'

'Closed in? Barty?'

'You never know what he's really thinking. At least I don't. He's all smooth on top, and nice, and great company, and when I was so upset about Clive he was absolutely sweet, but his real deep feelings never come out. Or maybe they do with you.'

Through the wine, I tried to focus. I knew Barty well, but I couldn't predict him on this. Last year when he thought I'd slept with my old boyfriend Peter (which I hadn't) he'd been angry. I supposed he had, because although he hadn't said anything he'd flounced off in a pique. We'd never talked it through, though, because so many other more urgent things happened that the question got buried.

What would he do about Carl? 'Never mind,' I said. 'He's not going to find out.'

'You're safe enough if Carl's in Chicago. What does he look like?'

I described him. 'He sounds like Johnny Depp,' she said.

'The problem is, he isn't,' I said.

'Isn't like Johnny Depp?'

'Isn't in Chicago. He's in London.'

'Oh,' said Polly.

Sunday, 3 April

Chapter Twenty

I woke up at five with a medium hangover, knowing I wasn't about to go back to sleep.

After thirty minutes, two paracetamols, three glasses of water, two cups of coffee and a shower I felt at a loose end. Not only was it too early to ring or visit anyone, but it was also Easter Sunday, as the silent and empty streets outside testified.

I had the day to myself. Nick was in Oxfordshire with Grace. Polly was going to her parents in the country, Barty to lunch with his brother's family in Holland Park. I'd been asked to that as well but I sure as heck wasn't going to join posh family knees-ups until I'd married into the posh family. If then.

I checked through my action list.

> see Abraham Master re sighting of Jacob, any other
>   info (?Tubbies' finances)
> ?Chicago for Eng Lit
> the loop
> Sandra Balmer true/false? motive if lying?
> Balmer Leisure Services, 2 Copthorne Square, Queen's
>   Park

merchant bank stuff – Nick
Jams ?any more secrets
grandparents: ring/visit ?father

Time I thought some more about 'the loop'. It could be metaphorical, as Barty'd thought. It now seemed more likely to me that Jacob had been referring to something specific to do with his adoption, maybe his biological mother, but I couldn't guess what.

When in doubt, look it up. I took my biggest dictionary from the shelf over my desk, and as I settled down with it at the kitchen table thought with a pang of premature nostalgia that soon, when the reference CD-ROMS I had on order arrived, I'd be using the computer for this.

Not knowing it was a redundant technology, the dictionary obligingly disgorged its information. A loop could be a round or oval shape formed by a line, any round or oval shaped thing that is closed or nearly closed, a piece of material curved round and fastened to form a ring or handle, or an intra-uterine contraceptive device. It was an aerial, a flight manoeuvre, a branch line for trains, or a term in electronics for closed circuits. In maths and physics it was a closed curve on a graph or an antinode. In anatomy it was a major pattern found in fingerprints and a shape in a kidney tubule. In computers it was a series of instructions performed repeatedly until a specific condition is satisfied. In skating it was a jump.

For one little word, it sure got about a bit. It would have been a lot easier if Jacob had said that the real him was in something unique and concrete, even if large, like the Grand Canyon. But one thing was obvious. Because 'the loop' described such a commonly occurring shape, it would be used in the jargon of plenty of subject areas that the dictionary hadn't caught. Barty had given me two: a dubbing loop and the inner circle of a government decision-making process.

If I kept asking different people, I'd get it eventually. But even when I'd got it, I wouldn't necessarily know.

I pinned up my loop notes on the action board, put the dictionary back and thought.

Balmer Leisure Services in Queen's Park. I could look round there, see what I could see. It'd surely be closed so I could snoop.

Maybe I should jog to Queen's Park.

No I couldn't, get real, my brain already felt too big for my skull and that was while I stood still.

If Polly was still asleep, I could borrow her car without asking. I took the spare set of car keys and went, gingerly, downstairs and out into the chilly street, then looked up at her windows. No sign of life. Good.

Queen's Park is an odd area, not one I know well. It's only about two miles from Notting Hill so it's definitely London. Some of its semi-detached Edwardian villas sit gloomily in tree-lined squares pretending to be top-of-the-range suburban, while just two streets away jerry-built dark cramped terrace houses in multiple occupation look too exhausted for pretence of any kind.

Balmer Leisure Services was at the top of the local heap. Number 2 Copthorne Square, the address I had, was a double-fronted red-brick Edwardian villa on three floors, complete with bay windows, little gables and a narrow surrounding strip of lawn and rhododendron bushes. It stood alone opposite the narrow end of a wedge-shaped communal garden, the sort where all the residents have keys, and dogs and children aren't allowed. I parked next to the garden, opposite the house, and scoped it out.

It was in good repair, neat, and utterly uncommunicative because all the windows were shuttered on the inside, with the kind of white metal security shutter you pull down and lock, not the picturesque wooden folding sort.

The street, the whole area, was empty of people as you'd expect at seven in the morning on Easter Sunday. I got out of the car, crossed the road and walked casually past the house. If there was anybody inside, I wouldn't know, so I didn't push my luck and go up the path. There was a small respectable polished brass plate by the rose-pink front door, with lettering too small for me to read.

I walked round the square while I was at it. The sun had come up but behind grey clouds so, while it wasn't dark, it wasn't very light either, and there was a cold breeze. I began to wake up properly and looked at the other houses as I passed. They were all semi-detached and solid. If they'd been in Hampstead they'd have been worth a fortune, and even here they wouldn't be cheap, and their owners were taking good care of them.

A respectable middle-class residential square. What kind of leisure services was Sandra Balmer's company providing for the neighbours? Or were the neighbours nothing to do with it? Had the company just happened to pick on the house as a head office? It didn't look like an office.

By now I'd almost lapped the square and had nearly reached the car, when I saw someone going up the front path of Number Two. A shabby woman, not old, not young, with a weary walk, two large carrier bags and a push-chair with a baby.

When she reached the door she put down her carrier bags and fumbled in her overcoat pocket. Eventually she found keys, a large heavy set of keys, and used three of them on the front door. When it opened she went straight in, leaving the baby outside, and then re-appeared, presumably having switched off the alarm system, looked across and saw me.

I got into the car, started it up and drove away.

I didn't think she'd noticed me. I hoped she hadn't. She didn't look interested, anyway.

She was the cleaner, surely, arriving at that time of the morning with a baby.

I wished I'd had Nick with me, then Nick could have kept her talking on some pretext – water for the car radiator, perhaps, or a telephone call to a car breakdown service – while I had a quick nose around the building.

Too late now. But I could try it with Barty tomorrow.

Not much wiser, and suddenly feeling bored and tired, I went back home to bed.

The telephone woke me but I let the answering machine catch it. By the time I went downstairs, the caller had rung off.

Nine-thirty. I opened the french windows to get some air and let the wind wake me properly. I don't like second sleeps, they make me irritable.

Then I listened to the message.

'Happy Easter, Alex! This is Sandra. Sandra Balmer. Please call me back, dear, as soon as you can. We must talk.'

Ring ring ring ring ring ring. Perhaps she was out, or in the sprawling bungalow's west wing. Finally, a pickup.

'This is Alex Tanner.'

'Thank you for calling so promptly, dear. I wonder . . . Have you been in touch with poor Jams?'

'Of course.'

'Is she still in America?'

'No.'

Pause. Laugh, the other end. 'She must have been delighted to hear that Jacob was safe. Though she's hurt, I expect? That he hadn't been in touch?'

Since I hadn't told Jams about Sandra, I'd have to come up with some lie but I wasn't sure what. Go for the obvious. 'Very hurt.'

'Aaah. I'm so sorry. Does she intend to take any further action?'

'That depends,' I said.

Pause. 'Alex, can we speak frankly?'

'I can,' I lied.

'You might have guessed I wasn't absolutely honest with you the other evening.'

'Yes.' Let her scramble for it, I thought. She's on a damage-limitation exercise, but why? Why not let her preposterous story about Kyrgyzstan simmer and wait to see if it erupted in her face?

'Jacob isn't travelling abroad.'

'Isn't he?'

'The poor boy . . . He's in a bad way. He had a breakdown.'

'A mental breakdown?'

'Yes. And you can see that he mustn't be upset, it's very important. Any contact with Jams would be very distressing for him.'

'That's possible,' I said. 'Why don't I have a word with him?'

'He's institutionalised,' said Sandra.

'I could visit the institution. So long as it isn't in Kyrgyzstan.'

Laugh. 'Of course not, it's in London.' Pause. 'That might be best,' she said. 'When?'

'Today?'

'But it's Easter Sunday! Oooh, you are a hard worker, aren't you, determined and ambitious. That's the way, I always used to tell my girls. Work hard and you'll get on.'

'What was your business, Sandra?'

'Leisure. That's the way forward in a post-industrial society, you know, the service industries and the media. You're so wise in your choice of career. But I do worry about you. Does your mum worry about you?'

'Sometimes,' I said, remembering my mother's furrowed face and her anxious question to Eddy about me, 'Who took care of her?'

'I would. Investigation can be dangerous, surely.'

Her tone was still sweet and light, but she was threatening me. 'I expect so,' I said non-committally.

'And that doesn't bother you?'

'It bothers me. It doesn't stop me.'

'Ah.' Pause. 'You're a practical girl?'

'Yes.'

'Financially speaking?'

'Yes,' I said.

'So a bit of money always comes in handy?'

'I hardly ever say no to money,' I said. 'Not real money. What are we talking about?'

Pause. 'Bottom line, ten thousand, in the hand and not a word to our friends at the Revenue.'

Ten thousand, first offer. That meant she'd go to twenty thousand.

Not a huge sum. But a much bigger sum than I could imagine being worth Sandra's while to pay just to get me off Jacob's back, or her own.

There was something fundamental I was missing about Jacob Stone.

'I'll have to think about it,' I said. 'Can I ring you back?'

'Oh do, you'd be so wise. I knew we'd understand each other,' she said with a gush of cosy relief. 'I'm out for lunch but I'll be back after four.'

'I'll ring you then,' I said. 'And Sandra . . .'

'Yes?'

'I always pay my taxes. It's a citizen's duty. So we'd have to allow for that. Round up proportionately.'

'Surely not if it's cash?'

'Tip-offs to the Revenue have been known.'

'Not by me,' said Sandra indignantly. 'Surely we can trust each other?'

'I'm sure we can, But you wouldn't want me to go against my conscience.'

Chapter Twenty-One

I put Liszt's second concerto on the CD, ground beans, made some of my best coffee, sat at the kitchen table and sipped. A possible twenty thousand pounds. That was serious. That was chilling. It gave substance to Sandra's implied threat of danger to me.

But what danger? What could she do?

It depended who she was, or what she was, and who her low-life contacts were, because she probably wasn't reckoning to do me any damage herself. My best guess was that she had been a madam of some kind, because she kept referring to her girls. Was Balmer Leisure Services an escort agency? If so, the house was too big just to be offices, surely, and escort agencies didn't usually provide bed space: too much trouble with the law.

It couldn't be a massage parlour. Wrong place, wrong presentation, no passing trade, and the neighbours would have raised hell.

Drug-dealing was the other possibility. If it was drugs, then I'd back off sharpish. Drugs meant huge profits, and crackheads, and guns. But it didn't fit with the house. Drug-dealers dealt on the streets, with mobile phones, and their bosses didn't hang around Queen's Park, they were in Jersey or Marseilles or Amsterdam or Miami.

The house was the key. Roll on seven o'clock tomorrow morning, when I could nip in and check it out.

But meanwhile I'd bought myself some time. Whether she had any intention of paying me I didn't know and didn't care, because I couldn't take the money. I'd have to speak to Jams and warn her that we might both be in big trouble, and see if there was anything else crucial she hadn't told me.

I poured some more coffee and fetched the telephone to the kitchen table. I'd just found Jams' number and was stretching out my hand to dial when the phone rang, startling me.

'Yes?' I said irritably.

'Alex Tanner?' An unfamiliar, educated male voice.

'Yes.'

'Patrick Brownlow here, Miss Tanner. We haven't met, but Mrs Balmer asked me to speak to you about one of my patients. I'm a consultant psychiatrist, in attendance part-time at the Caritas Clinic.'

'Is this about Jacob?'

'Yes, but I'd prefer not to discuss it over the telephone. Perhaps we might meet? I could come to you, if that would be more convenient?'

'When?'

'Today?'

An eminent psychiatrist, offering to make a house call on Easter Sunday? The stakes were upping all the

time. I'd heard of Patrick Brownlow. He was a very top
persons' shrink, and the Caritas was a very top persons' place. If a minor member of the Royal Family or
a film star jolted off their trolley or stuck their nose
too far into the candy, off to the Caritas with them.

'Of course,' I said, of course. 'What time?'

'Would noon suit you?'

'Fine.'

He was exactly on time. A distinguished-looking man,
about fifty, with an attractive irregular face and thick
dark just-greying hair combed straight back from his
forehead. He was wearing a light tweed suit that
looked as if it had come from a good tailor and made
him look slimmer and taller. He was actually about
five foot eight and on the blocky side.

He came in, made appreciative noises about my
flat and about me sparing the time, and accepted a
cup of coffee. He was surprisingly pleasant. Psy-
chiatrists in my experience (and I've known a lot of
of them, through my mother) are either neurotic or
power-freaks. He didn't appear to be either, and he
chatted amiably about the weather and about the
music I was playing (Mahler) for the right length of
time.

Then he came to the point. Jacob was his patient,
had been since last October when Sandra had brought
him in. He couldn't of course discuss the details of the
case but Jacob was very unwell and had been in
the Caritas ever since. He, Brownlow, wanted to

reassure me and my unfortunate client that Jacob was indeed alive, that nothing physical had happened to him, but that a meeting with Jams at this stage wouldn't be helpful. Might even be damaging. And a meeting with me would be equally so because I was representing Jams.

'You could always tell him I wanted to see him for some other reason. We could make it up,' I said.

He shook his head. 'I never lie to my patients,' he said. 'Never. Most of them are my patients because too many people have told them lies in the past, or continue to do so.'

'That's the neurotics, I suppose. So Jacob's a neurotic, not a psychotic?' I fished.

He smiled and said nothing.

I smiled too. I liked him. He was quietly clever and he had an expressive face. But just because I liked him, I wasn't going to let him get away with anything. 'So what's your association with Sandra Balmer?' I said, 'Why did she bring Jacob to you in the first place? Especially all the way down here from Doncaster?'

'I've known Sandra for years. She trusts me,' he said.

'She's an unusual person,' I said. 'What's her line of business?'

He raised one dark eyebrow. 'Leisure services, I believe.'

'What's that?'

'I've no idea.'

'Doesn't that bother you?'

He smiled. 'Not at all,' he said. 'She's not my patient.'

'When do you think Jacob will be well enough to talk to Jams?'

'That's difficult to say.'

'Does he feel anything for her at all? Does he love her?'

He shook his head. 'I can't answer you,' he said. 'I can't discuss my patient.'

'So what do I tell Jams?'

'Tell her what I've told you. The rest is up to her.'

'She loves him. I know it sounds silly after just one meeting, but I think she actually does. Deeply.'

'Then I am sorry,' he said, and he sounded as if he really was.

'Should I encourage her to hope that when he's better he'll want to see her?'

He looked at his hands, which were lightly clasped on his knee. 'I'm not sure that would be a good idea,' he said, finally, carefully.

I trusted him instinctively, but I didn't trust Sandra, and he was her messenger. Even so I hesitated. Should I tell him about the baby? That might jolt him into more confidences. But then again he might tell Sandra, and since I didn't know what was going on, I didn't know whether the fact of her pregnancy might expose Jams to danger. It made her more vulnerable, somehow.

No, I wouldn't. 'So you think she's lost him?' I said. 'She should drop it? Behave as if she'd never met him?'

'If she can, that would be best,' he said.

I met his eyes. He was telling me Jacob was dead, I thought. That's what he was saying. And not meta- phorically, either, not mentally ill and beyond Jams' reach, but actually dead.

I didn't understand why he'd agreed to see me. I couldn't begin to guess what pressure Sandra, or someone bigger than Sandra, had put on him to make him do this. I trusted the man, but his mission stank.

I couldn't think of anything else to ask. 'Thanks, then,' I said. He got up to go and I walked down the stairs with him. We'd said our goodbyes and I was closing the street door when something struck me. He wouldn't answer, but I might get a reaction. I called 'Wait!'

He turned on the steps.

'The loop.'

'I'm sorry?'

'Any idea what Jacob could have meant when he said that the real him was in the loop?'

'Did he say that?'

'To Jams.'

'The loop,' he said consideringly. 'No, I'm sorry. It means nothing to me.'

Chapter Twenty-Two

As soon as Brownlow left, I called Jams. I couldn't any longer justify keeping anything from her. We needed to meet, and talk the case through. The answering machine was on. I asked her to pick up but there was no response so I left a call-back message.

Then I rang Grace Macarthy's cottage in Oxfordshire. It sounded like a good party. I could hear noises and laughter in the background and the receiver was passed from hand to hand until I finally got Nick.

'I need you tomorrow morning, early. About six. Can you get a lift back tonight?'

'Wait.'

More noise and laughter. Then she came back.

'OK,' she said.

I hesitated, briefly. Should I offer her a bed for the night? She was doing me a favour by interrupting her stay with Grace. No. She had a perfectly good foster-home to go to, if she chose. If I once let her stay, I'd never get rid of her.

She read my mind. 'I can stay at Grace's,' she said, 'see you,' and rang off.

It was now nearly one o'clock on Easter Sunday

and unlike most of the British population I didn't have to go anywhere for a family lunch. That satisfactory thought in itself finally banished my hangover. I felt well enough to run, and I knew I should, because while I ran maybe my subconscious would come up with a pattern for the confusing and conflicting information I had.

At this stage of a case, thinking about it didn't help. It had to shake down and simmer.

As I changed into my jogging gear and my new top-of-the-range Nike trainers, something struck me. Family lunch. My grandparents. They'd be at home, bound to be. Unless I had great-aunts and great-uncles, but somehow I didn't think so, not close ones anyway because if they had been surely they'd have helped my mother out when she was pregnant with me?

Or maybe not. I didn't know, but it was time I found out, and the four or so miles round trip to Ealing was a reasonable run.

I found the Tanners' address, checked out the road in my A–Z, and set off before I could reconsider.

Good running weather. Still chilly, but not wet. I headed west and set a good pace. Posh residential streets. Aspiring residential streets. Narrow ex-railway workers' cottage streets. Past Wormwood Scrubs prison, over a main shopping road, temporarily deserted, into the wilderness of huge hangar-like DIY stores, over the railway, through the industrial bleakness of Acton, into the small suburban streets of Ealing, to a sports ground.

Then I stopped to get my breath. It was opposite here, somewhere, in a maze of crescents. I started again, more slowly, weaving my way in and out of the cul-de-sacs of smallish semi-detached 1930s houses, each with their front gate and carefully tended patch of front garden, many with individual number-plaques, some with names.

There it was. No 24 Malvern Crescent, my ancestral home. Sprucely kept. The front garden was gravel: low-maintenance. There was a small bay tree in a tub beside the dark red front door, under the overhanging porch. The tub was chained to the porch. The tree didn't look as if it was planning a getaway: it looked disheartened.

I looked down the street. Empty of people. Everyone inside, trying to be a happy family. At least I'd never had to do that.

The door was answered on the second ring. 'Yes?' said the old man irritably. He was tallish, not much bent by age, with iron-grey hair around a bald-patch, a long face with a rather fine hooked nose and brown eyes. He looked as if he thought himself a fine figure of a man. His leather brogues were well-polished, his cavalry twill trousers spruce, his white shirt clean, his tie unspotted. He was wearing a heavy hand-knitted green cardigan with leather buttons.

'John Tanner?' I said.

'Yes. You've interrupted our lunch, whoever you are. Please state your business.'

His accent surprised me. Accents place you, in England. In your class, in your region, in your edu-

THE LOOP

cation, in your age-group. I use two: the sloppy semi-cockney I picked up from my mates, and Received Standard. I'd expected his to be suburban London. It wasn't. It was BBC would-be upper-class English of fifty years ago, the kind of voice that announced the rescue of our troops by the brave little boats at Dunkirk.

'Who is it? John, who is it?' called a voice from inside. This accent was different. Country Irish. My grandmother was Irish. Maureen, a Catholic, of course.

'I'm trying to find out,' he snapped over his shoulder.

'Shall I put your meal back in the oven to keep warm?'

'Do what you like,' he called, then turned back to me. 'Now, Miss Whoever-you-are, unless you have something to say I'm going to close this door. Good day to you.'

I put my foot squarely across the lintel. 'My name is Alex Tanner,' I said. His face went still, as if he was thinking, then he pushed the door further closed so it squeezed my foot, painfully. I didn't move.

'John? Who is it? John? Your food's getting cold.'

'It's Alex Tanner,' I called. 'Your grand-daughter.'

'Oh,' said the voice from the interior. 'Oh. John?'

'What do you want?' said my grandfather.

'Information,' I said.

'A fine time to choose,' he said. 'I suppose you want some lunch, as well.'

'No, thank you.'

'Do you expect me to believe that? Arriving at lunchtime? You won't get any money out of us, either.'

'I just want information,' I said conciliatingly.

'Hrumpff,' he said. The noise expressed irritation, knowingness, self-righteousness and male superiority. That's how it struck me, anyhow.

I nearly lost my temper. 'I just want information,' I said sweetly. 'If you don't let me in I'll take my clothes off in the front garden and scream until all the neighbours come out to look. Grandpa.'

I followed him in. She began to lay an extra place for me without speaking to me, then when he snapped she took the extra place away and they both kept on eating. Roast beef and yorkshire pudding and roast potatoes and mashed potatoes and cauliflower and carrots and peas and gravy and horseradish and mustard, served in myriad dishes on mats on a polished dining-table in a small dining-room with dark-red velvet curtains with pelmets and red and white striped wallpaper and small heavy-framed landscape watercolours on the walls and a dark-red Turkish carpet with brown patterned shapes on the floor.

She looked like my mother, but older and saner. Pretty. Neat. Well turned out, in a dark blue jacket and grey pleated skirt and powder-blue jersey. She didn't meet my eye but she kept glancing sideways at him.

They didn't offer me a chair, but I moved one from its place against the wall and brought it up to the table.

When I sat down Maureen looked at me as if my track-suited bum would contaminate her furniture.

My grandfather had a point, it had been a bad time to pick, but then I hadn't been considering their feelings. I still wasn't, much. They hadn't earned consideration. And I didn't seem to be putting them off their food.

Still . . . 'I'm sorry to interrupt your lunch, but I won't stay long. I just want to know the name of my father. Oh, and a bit about the family health.'

'We have nothing to say to you,' he said.

'The quicker you tell me, the quicker I'll go.'

'My family have always been healthy,' he said. 'Maureen?'

She shook her head and kept eating.

'Maureen's family are healthy too,' he said.

'So what do they die of?' I said. 'Or do they live forever?'

'Heart attacks. Strokes. At a good age. Mustard, please, Maureen.'

He could have reached the mustard himself. Either he liked being waited on, or he was nervous. It didn't matter. 'No mental illness? On either side?'

'Of course not. And Susan was never mentally ill.'

'No, she wasn't,' said my grandmother. 'She was just upset.'

'Guilty,' said my grandfather. 'And rightly so, after what she had done. I told the social worker, but she wouldn't listen. Susan didn't need a psychiatrist. She needed discipline.'

'And the comfort of the church,' said Maureen. 'More gravy, John?'

'Not now,' he said irritably.

I wanted out of there. 'My father's name,' I said. 'Please.'

He took the nearly full bottle of red wine from its little silver coaster and poured a little into her half-full glass, more into his empty one. He had a nervous tic at the corner of one eye. Perhaps it was stress. Perhaps he always had. I'd never know.

I'd give him just a bit more time. I looked around at the room, so neat and polished and well-kept. So much effort. I supposed my grandmother did the housework. The wallpaper and the painting looked professionally done, and he didn't strike me as the DIY type. So what did he do, now he was retired from being a clerk in the town hall? He dressed and spoke as if his background had aimed him further up the pecking-order than that, anyway. Why hadn't he made it?

'Please tell me,' I said again.

'Why? So you can make a scene like this?'

This was a scene?

'I'll probably just ring him up. I need to know about his health.'

'Why?'

'I have my own reasons.'

'I cannot condone any disruption of his life. Susan behaved very badly.'

'She knew better,' said my grandmother. 'We'd

196

taught her better. And he's an important man now. Don't go upsetting him.'

'Maureen,' said my grandfather warningly. She coughed nervously.

'You'd better tell me. I'm a television researcher. And a private investigator. I find things out for a living. All I have to do is go through the school staff list for thirty years ago, and that'll make more trouble.'

My grandfather's tic speeded up.

'Right, I'll find out myself,' I said, and stood up.

'His name is Alexander. William Alexander.'

'And what's important about him?'

'He's a headmaster,' said Maureen, proudly.

On the run back, I set the pace for twelve minute miles. I felt nothing for my grandparents. For my mother, I felt sorrow, and for myself, relief. I couldn't have grown up in that house with those people, not the me whose feet pounded the pavements in Nike trainers, not the me who couldn't wait to get back on to the Stone case. I'd have grown sideways like Sandra Balmer's bungalow, or not grown at all, like a bonsai.

Next stop, my father. William Alexander. My mother must have loved him, to give me his name. Or perhaps she hadn't worked out that although later she might want to forget him, she'd be reminded every time she spoke to me.

Now I was being stupid. She'd have been reminded anyway, every time she looked at me. That was the trouble with children, they didn't go away.

Once you had them, they were permanent reminders of the circumstances of their conception.

And all the time I was getting closer to having to give Barty an answer. Having a child with him would be irrevocable. I could never finish the paperwork on that, send an invoice and bank the cheque. In the normal course of things, it would be the other way round; the child would bury me and file my will for probate and bank the cheque.

Enough, already.

Chapter Twenty-Three

'How about I buy you some more pillows?' said Barty, trying to fold his entitlement of one so it propped him comfortably.

'The aftermath of passion should make you indifferent to physical comfort,' I said, slapping his thieving hand away from my pillow.

'It has for some months. Now it isn't.'

'Are you going off me? Didn't you enjoy it?' I said, sounding more anxious than I wanted, feeling more anxious than I wanted.

'Very much . . . I'm not going off you. Only your lack of bedding, which one trip to Peter Jones would secure.' He hugged me reassuringly.

I wanted reassurance but I didn't want to be reassured. 'D'you want some water?' I said, wriggling away.

'Thanks.'

I passed him a bottle of Tesco own-brand water. I have tried, but I can't drink it from the tap. 'I saw my grandparents today.'

He went still. 'Oh?'

'But I've got to see my father, yet.'

'Right.'

'I just wanted you to know that I'm doing what I said I would.'

'I never doubted it. How were your grandparents?'

'Rather sad.' I kissed his shoulder.

'Mmmm,' he said appreciatively. 'What time is it?'

I squinted at the clock. Nearly six . . . I've got to get up and make a phone call in a minute.'

'D'you want to tell me about it?'

'What?'

'Your grandparents. Your phone call. The case.'

'Not right now.'

'D'you and Polly want to come over this evening? I'll cook some chops.'

'What about Magnus?'

'I've never cooked a magnus.'

'Ha ha,' I said, and hit him with my pillow.

He took it and put it behind his head.

'Snake,' I said. No point in trying to get it back, he was much too strong. And quick. I lay flat on the bed. 'Get me some pillows, then, if it means so much to you. And Polly and I are having an Indian takeaway in front of the telly, thanks, so no thanks.'

As soon as the door closed behind him I was on the phone to Jams again. Still the answering machine, still no pickup. She might have gone away for the Bank Holiday, might not be back until Tuesday, or later. Why hadn't I asked her where she'd be?

Never mind. I'd stall Sandra.

'Alex Tanner here.'

'Hello, my dear.'

'Sandra, I saw Patrick Brownlow.'

'Isn't he a nice man?'

'Very.'

'Did he set your mind at rest?'

Difficult. I couldn't sound too convinced, because she'd offered me money. Silence money. Which meant that I hadn't necessarily been expected to believe what Brownlow said. Presumably he'd been sent to give me a conscience sweetener, a reason for declaring myself satisfied, maybe even a reason to tell Jams I'd actually seen Jacob.

'Up to a point,' I said.

'What point would that be?'

'I don't know until I've talked to my client. She's away at the moment and I'm not sure when she'll be back.'

'What will you be telling her?'

None of her business, of course. I hesitated, then decided that the more safely bought I sounded, the safer I'd be, for the moment. 'That Jacob is mentally ill but safe at the Caritas Clinic. That I don't know when he'll recover. That she'd do best to write him off to experience, for his sake as much as hers.'

Silence the other end. Had I been too glib? 'And is that what you think, my dear?'

'Oh, yes. Better all round. Looking at it from a practical point of view.'

'I'm so glad you think so,' said Sandra warmly.

'I'll be in touch as soon as I've spoken to Jams. So we can firm up the arrangements.'

After I'd showered and dressed, I headed back to the kitchen and the action-board. I had a nagging feeling I'd forgotten something, and I needed to update the action list anyhow, before Polly came back from the country and I had to concentrate on her.

I looked at the list.

> *see Abraham Master re sighting of Jacob, any other*
>   *info (?Tubbies' finances)*
> *?Chicago for Eng Lit*
> *?the loop*
> *Sandra Balmer true/false? motive if lying?*
> *BLS, 2 Copthorne Square, Queen's Park*
> *merchant bank stuff – Nick*
> *Jams ?any more secrets*
> *grandparents: ring/visit ?father*
> *ring Carl about Monday – ?letters*

Not many changes to make. I crossed off *true/false* from the Sandra item – her information was certainly false – and added *?Brownlow motive*. I changed the second last entry to

   William Alexander – ring/see

and avoided the thought that the next change I made to the last slot might be to insert *Barty – decide*.

Then I rang Carl. He was in. He sounded pleased to hear me, annoyed that I hadn't rung earlier, and eager to see me the next day. I agreed to meet him at his hostel at ten, and then we'd go out for coffee. I didn't want him anywhere near my flat, and I wanted to be clear of him early enough to get up to Doncaster and see Master in the afternoon.

Then I sat down with a cup of coffee and Nick's notes on the merchant bank. Catterstone Almack's, it was called. I'd heard of it, but knew nothing about it, which didn't mean much because I've never worked on a City or economics programme so it might have been a household name in the Square Mile, for all I knew. Nick's notes gave me a background on the bank, which I skimmed, and then two telephone numbers. One in Nick's neat characterless writing, the central bank number, the other in Grace's scrawl – with a comment – *if you want, try Sir Malise Douglas – a good friend of mine and a director – use my name – this is his home number – or I'll call him if you like.*

My knee-jerk reaction was of annoyance at Grace. Typical of her to have a director who was a good friend.

Then I turned my annoyance inwards. Typical of me to be unproductively envious. What did it matter who Grace knew? If this man could be useful, then I'd use him.

But I'd try the central number first. Tomorrow.

Monday, 4 April

Chapter Twenty-Four

Plan A was for me to hide round the side of the house at 2 Copthorne Square and Nick to loiter in the road. When the cleaner arrived, unlocked the door and switched off the alarm, Nick would distract her for three minutes while I slipped into the house, had a quick look round, and slipped out again.

There wasn't a Plan B.

I was in position at a quarter to seven so I had plenty of time, standing pressed against the side of the house, to imagine what could go wrong.

The Neighbourhood Watch could spot me and ring the police.

The Neighbourhood Watch could spot Nick and ring the police.

There might be someone in the house. It didn't look like it and I didn't think so, but there might.

The cleaner might not work on Bank Holidays, especially as she'd already worked on Easter Sunday.

Nick might not succeed in distracting the cleaner. She hadn't told me what pretext she was going to use. 'Trust me,' she'd said, and for that kind of street-kid scam, I did.

7.05. No cleaner. It was raining, had been since we'd got there. Steady, heavy rain. My jeans were soaked and though my leather bomber jacket was just about coping, great splodges of water from a blocked gutter above overflowed every so often, drenching my head and trickling down my neck.

7.07. She was coming up the path. I kept absolutely still. I could see the path near the gate but when she got closer to the front door she was out of my field of view. No sign of Nick yet. I could hear the locks turning, the door opening, then see Nick moving up the path.

Nothing for a moment, then Nick again, legging it down the path with the push-chair, complete with baby. She was ten yards down the street by the time the cleaner screamed and ran after her.

I'd have to speak to Nick about pulling such a cruel gag, but not now with my 180 seconds clicking away. Right now I was in through the front door and up the stairs.

There was a child-gate at the top. Why? Think later. As my wet fingers fiddled with the catch, I looked down into the hall. There were no lights on, but in the daylight from the partly open front door I could see that all the other doors leading off it were shut.

Through the child-gate, on to the landing. Almost totally dark now. Corridor to the right and the left. I went left, reached a door, had my hand on the knob, then jumped away. A noise. The noise of a flushing toilet, inside.

Flush a toilet, leave the bathroom.

I darted back across the landing and opened the first door I came to, went in, shut it behind me.

It was absolutely dark. I could see nothing at all. The security shutters, I supposed, plus curtains.

I listened hard. Nothing I could hear from the corridor. Maybe it was an en-suite bathroom. I hoped so. If whoever it was turned a light on in the corridor they'd certainly see my wet footprints. Or maybe not. Most people aren't at their best just after seven in the morning.

When I stopped listening, I was aware of the smell. Powerful, sweet, familiar. A childhood smell.

Vanilla.

I reckoned I had a minute and a half left. I didn't want to switch on a light in case it showed under the door. I'd get some night-sight soon, surely.

I dropped to my hands and knees and groped my way into the centre of the room. Thick carpet. Ah – wood. A chair or table leg, about three inches in diameter. I ran my hand up it, feeling it narrow. And up. And up, until I was standing, my hand about five feet from the ground, and still no seat or table-top. A head-height plant stand?

Ah. A horizontal piece of wood. I ran my hand across it. Smooth, polished, about three foot by three foot, with narrow vertical spokes of wood at the back and the sides.

I had to stand on tip-toe to reach the narrow piece of wood on top of the spokes.

What the hell was it?

Two minutes. At least.

I went for the door, felt the wall beside it on the left.

Nothing.

Felt the wall on the right.

Light switch. Click.

In the sudden flood of light, I saw two things.

The first was the object I'd been touching, an adult-size baby's high chair. So I knew what Balmer Leisure Services did.

The second was an adult-size baby's cot. Occupied. And I didn't have the faintest idea what I was going to do.

I switched off the light.

The occupant of the cot was asleep, I thought. His eyes had been closed. Maybe he was dead. I couldn't hear him breathing, but the cot was the other side of the room, about twelve feet away.

Given the choice, I'd have gone for dead, because alive and awake he'd be a monster, the kind of man a sumo wrestler would take on double-dates to make him look slim and handsome. My one glimpse of him had made a deep impression. Naked except for underpants, short, but wider than he was high, built like a prop-forward, as my rugby-mad ex-boyfriend Peter would have said. Come back, Peter, all is forgiven. If Cot wasn't a rugby player he had been a boxer, or he'd lost lots of arguments, because although he had two ears, two eyes, a nose and a mouth, they'd been shuffled and dealt several times. Plus he had a very low forehead and his body was matted with hair. It was only an informed guess that he was human.

I heard him stir.

Go, now.

As I tensed my muscles to move I heard footsteps in the corridor.

Then the door opened. By a fluke, I was behind it, so even though the light went on, whoever'd come in couldn't see me.

But Cot could, and he was waking up. Slowly. And looking towards me.

'Yer what?' he said.

'Goo-goo-goo-goo,' said the man in the doorway, and he moved just a little further into the room.

He looked like Cot's wider uglier hairier older brother, and he was wearing a giant terry nappy fastened with giant blue nappy pins, and sucking at a giant baby-bottle. 'Goo-goo-goo,' he said again. 'Geddit? Goo-goo-goo.'

He hadn't seen me yet, but Cot had, and he pointed at me.

Nappy turned, saw me, and goggled.

All I knew about Sandra's kind of leisure services I'd learned from a late-night Eurodoco about a brothel in Germany which had sent me to sleep half-way through, but I had to give it a whirl. He was blocking my way out.

'Now now, time for bath and bed,' I said coyly. 'Which dirty little boy needs his botty spanked?'

211

'What the bluddy 'ell?' Nappy said, broad Yorkshire.

'Nanny has to get her uniform first,' I said wagging my finger and edging past him.

'Hang on a mo,' he said. 'Don't get t'wrong idea, lass.'

'It's her,' said Cot. He was Yorkshire too.

'Hang on,' said Nappy, and took hold of my arms. 'Don't get t'wrong idea. I worn't serious, like.'

He was stronger than he looked. After an initial wriggle I kept quite still.

'It's her. Short lass wi' big tits an' red hair an' boots,' persisted Cot, struggling ineffectually to lower the cot-side.

'You Alex Tanner?' said Nappy.

'Yes,' I said. 'Can I help you?'

'We want a word wi' you,' said Nappy. I wriggled experimentally, but he didn't loosen his grasp. He didn't seem hostile, however. I felt more foolish than scared, helpless in his grip with my feet inches off the floor.

'Not yet,' said Cot urgently and authoritatively. He was clearly the brains of the partnership. 'We gorra wait.'

'What do I do wi't'lass, then?' demanded Nappy.

Then Nick got him square in the balls, with an up-and-under kick from behind and his howl could have been heard up north.

'Go!' I said, and we legged it for the stairs with Nappy following, doubled up and moaning. The cleaner was standing by the foot of the stairs, hugging her baby. When we ran down she moved away, but as we reached the front door she screamed.

I turned to look, still moving.

She'd just seen Nappy at the top of the stairs.

Chapter Twenty-Five

I started the car and drove away, my heart still thumping from the sprint.

Nick was gleeful. 'It's a major design fault,' she said.

'What is?'

'Men's balls.'

Pause. Her high spirits subsided. Then she said, rather scornfully, 'What's the matter, Alex? Were you scared?'

'Some of the time.'

'So, what else? You'd been in there *ages*. Over six minutes, twice what we'd agreed. Didn't you want me in?'

'I wasn't in any danger, I don't think. But you weren't to know that.'

'So why are you annoyed with me?'

'I'm not annoyed with you. I'm annoyed with me, for making a very bad mistake.'

'Explain.'

I don't like explaining. It means going over, out loud, what one has already gone over in one's head, and I'd already had to bring Nick up to speed once that morning on the case so far. I took a deep breath and made it quick. 'We've found out what Sandra does. Sexual services in the baby line. We've found out that she's sent two men down south, after me.'

'How do you know they were after you?'

'Because they recognized me. They said my name. We've also got a possible reason for the psychiatrist to do what Sandra says.'

'Which is?'

'If he's a "powder-my-bum" man, he's not going to want it common knowledge. What kind of cred would he have? If she threatened—'

'Yeah, yeah, I get it,' she said impatiently. 'But what does she actually do? I've never heard of it.'

'Some men like being treated as babies. Fed, changed, bathed, baby-talked. Put in cots and high-chairs.'

'You mean they get off on that?'

'Yes.'

'Typical. Easy money for us, though.'

'Us?'

'Women.'

I concentrated on driving and waited for her to get back to the point.

It didn't take long. 'So what's the mistake?' she said. 'If we have all this information, and we're OK—'

'The mistake is what I've given away. Sandra might be a heavy-duty player. Chances are she is. She feels like one.'

'Those two gorillas didn't look serious to me. Not if they're into nappies.'

'I don't think they are into nappies. It was a joke, that bit. I think they were just kipping there overnight because it was a cheap and safe place for Sandra to put them while they're in town. The cleaner didn't expect them to be there, that's why she screamed. Oh, and never pull a trick like that again – pretending to kidnap a baby.'

'Why? It worked great.'

'It would. But it's over the top. I wanted a diversion, not world war three. You frightened her.'

'Anyway they didn't look serious,' said Nick stubbornly. 'Not real hard men. A bit of clumping, that looked their style.'

'What's clumping?'

'Putting the boot in. Breaking a leg. Throwing ammonia. Warning people off, teaching them a lesson.'

I reflected on that. On the whole, I thought she was right. But I wasn't as indifferent to being clumped as she seemed to be. Youth, that was it. She still thought of herself as immune, not just to death but also damage. I didn't. I'd had my leg broken once and I didn't want it to happen again, and although I hadn't felt threatened by Sandra's men then, I didn't think she'd told them to damage me. But she could.

'So go on, I still don't understand,' said Nick impatiently.

'Sandra thought I was going along with her. I hope. Which would give me time, without hassles, to keep working. But now she'll know for sure I'm not going along, because if I was, would I be poking around?'

When we got back to my flat, Barty was in the kitchen. He'd brought croissants and made coffee. 'You're both soaked,' he said. 'What've you been up to?'

I wasn't going to explain again. I let Nick do it.

When she'd finished, Barty said 'Mmm' and looked at me. I looked back. He couldn't think I'd been any stupider than I thought I'd been.

'You could have asked Eddy Barstow,' he said. 'The local police'll know all about Balmer Leisure. Two telephone calls would have sorted it.'

'Mmm,' I said, and went next door to put Liszt on the CD and listen to the only message on my answering machine. It was Jams, and she'd be in all morning.

When I got back, Barty said, 'Could we *not* have Liszt?'

'Why?'

'Too early in the morning.'

'Why?'

'He's like tiramisù. Too sweet altogether.'

'What's tiramisù?'

'Can I have a bath, Alex?' said Nick, wisely, stuffing a croissant into her mouth in one piece.

'Do,' I said.

She vanished up the stairs, as close to scuttling as I've ever seen her.

'What?' I said, standing square on to him, resisting the strong temptation to put my hands on my hips.

'Beethoven, perhaps? Or Mozart?'

'I'm not running Classic Requests here. What?'

'Let's don't fight.'

'Let's do.'

'Don't take your misjudgement out on me,' said Barty.

I gasped. 'I'm not,' I snapped.

He said nothing.

'Yes I am,' I said. 'OK, I am. But I don't have to like it.'

I sat down, buttered a croissant, let the Liszt fill my ears. He was right about that too: I heard it sweet.

'What'll you do?' he said.

'Keep on going,' I said. 'Warn Jams. Keep Nick out of harm's way. Hope I get to Sandra before she gets to me.'

He raised an eyebrow at me. 'Eddy?' he said.

'How, Eddy?'

'Tell Eddy.'

'He'd only fuss.'

'I'm worried,' he said.

'I know. Don't be. I can handle it.'

When he'd finished his breakfast, he went away.

That's one of his great charms for me. He does it a lot. But I think it was an effort for him, this time.

As the door closed behind him, Nick came downstairs. 'Coffee?' she said anxiously.

'I'm fine,' I said.

She topped up my mug, relieved. 'You don't want to get married, do you?'

'I don't know.'

'Then don't.'

'If I wanted a guidance counsellor—'

'You'd hire one, I know, I know. Are we going to work, or chat?'

'Work. Now.'

I cancelled my meeting with Carl, left Nick to try her luck with the merchant bank, and took a taxi over to Jams' place in South Kensington, keeping a sharp eye out in case Cot and Nappy were following me. No sign of a car, but I paid off the taxi two streets away and walked the rest, just in case.

It was a mews house, white-painted, bijou, with a delicate black wrought-iron and glass front door and pastel coloured little flowers in window-boxes. I've never learnt the names of flowers, but these looked as if they should have been called sweet-peas. The rain was flattening them.

Jams let me in, greeted me enthusiastically, took my jacket to hang up, and offered me camomile tea. I accepted, bravely, because I don't like tea-bag tea much and can hardly swallow herbal brews, and looked around the living-room while she was out making it for a strategic plant. All her plants were flowering, most of them were pink, some of them were fuchsias. I know fuchsias because Barty used to give me them until he spotted how quickly they died under my care.

The room was low-ceilinged, and the full narrow width of the house, with an open polished staircase leading up on the left. The furniture was smallish, and delicate, mostly antique or good repro, and the sofa was a two-seater upholstered in patterned cream damask with wooden legs. There were porcelain plates on the walls and a landscape in oils over the small marble mantelpiece.

'Nice place,' I said when she came back with two mugs.

'Glad you like it. Do sit down.'

I sat on the sofa, she sat on a matching chair. 'When did you buy?' I said, trying to price it in my head. Two hundred thousand in the falling market? Two-fifty at the peak of the boom?

'Oh, it isn't mine. It's rented. I rented it last December, for Jacob. I thought he'd like it as a London base. My own flat is much too small for both of us. There's a study upstairs for him, and the double bedroom, of course, though I did wonder about the ceilings being too low because he's very tall, but he could have stood up straight. Even in heels I can with inches to spare.'

So in December she was still, genuinely, expecting him to turn up. You wouldn't move for the convenience of someone you'd killed out of pique. And looking at Jams again with her neat plaited blonde hair and maternity jeans and big soft sweater, pale blue with kittens, and hearing her whispery little voice, I couldn't see her as the murderer. If we even had a corpse.

Then I took a deep breath and started to explain. I told her everything I'd found out and everyone I'd seen. I did it patiently, even when she took to repeating what I said as if we were in a *Learn English Painlessly in Three Months* tape. She had a lot to take in, after all.

The whole process took nearly half an hour and I was controlling myself so desperately that by the end I found I'd drunk the camomile tea.

'Well done, Alex,' she said finally. 'You've done a lot. And it was very brave of you to go into that house in north London.'

'Thanks,' I said. That was all I said. I don't point out my own mistakes to clients. 'Now I need your help.'

'Oh,' she said. 'How?'

'Bearing in mind what I've found out, have you anything more to tell me about your conversation with Jacob?'

'Like what?'

I took a deep breath. 'For instance, did he give any clues about who his real mother might be?'

'He didn't say his mother wasn't his mother.'

'But now we know she wasn't, does anything he said about "the real him" come to mind?'

'He said it was in the loop.'

'What did he say right after that?'

' "I love you", I think,' she said, tears welling. 'I don't think I can bear it. I've told you everything,

Alex, I really have, absolutely everything that could help. He thought what he was going to do might be dangerous and he was right, but he didn't want me to know about it and he didn't tell me any more. Really, really, you must believe me. You should, because I've been right all along. You thought I was making a fuss about nothing, that Jacob hadn't been serious. I knew he had. I knew it. And he told Carl about me, and Sandra, which shows our love was just as important to me as it was to him.'

'OK,' I said, more gently. Her baby-bump was pointed reproachfully at me and her fingers fluttered over it protectively. I couldn't see that asking a mother to think posed a threat to the unborn child, but I wasn't going to get anywhere, clearly. 'OK, Jams, I believe you. But now you have to decide what to do.'

'He's really dead,' she said with a fresh flow of tears.

'Maybe they just want us to think so.'

'Something horrible happened to him.'

'It needn't have been horrible. You're a Christian. Maybe he's just gone to join his Maker.'

She mopped her eyes with a little linen handkerchief trimmed with pink. She and Sandra had one thing in common: they both liked pastels. I didn't reckon that Sandra would see that as a powerful reason for laying off Jams, though, if she got in the way. 'We've got to think about you, now. You and the baby. I don't really know what's happened, but I'm sure Sandra could be dangerous. If I keep investigating, she'll trace you eventually and she may threaten you. If I stop, and do a deal with her, it's possible she might keep it, and that's the last we'd hear.'

'Do you want the money?' said Jams. 'The ten thousand pounds? Because I'd pay you that. If necessary.'

I wasn't offended. Polly'd probably told her I liked money, as of course I do. But I like my own way more. Much more.

'Forget the money,' I said. 'That's not an issue. You're the client, you decide.'

She patted her swelling kittened stomach. 'I want my baby to know his father loved his mother. *I* know it. I want my baby to know it too, to be able to say, Daddy didn't just dump Mummy. He did his best. He'd be here to watch me grow up, and to guide me and father me properly, if he could. I need to know what happened. You can protect me, Alex, can't you? Polly said you were tough. And clever.'

'That was kind of her. But there's tough and tough. I can't go up against heavy men, not physically. And I still haven't got the sense of this.'

'But you're on the way to finding out. You have more things to do, more people to see. You'll get there.'

She seemed absolutely unconcerned. 'I can't guarantee your safety,' I said bluntly. 'Oughtn't you to consider the baby?'

'I am. We are in God's hands, Alex. Me. And you. And my baby. We're all safe in God's hands. I'll get us some more camomile tea.'

Chapter Twenty-Six

'Bank's a dead loss,' said Nick. 'Only a skeleton staff in because it's a Bank Holiday, and none of them have ever heard of him, and none of them care either. I'll try again tomorrow.'

'I don't want to wait that long. We'll have to use Grace and her director,' I said.

Nick looked surprised. 'I didn't think you'd want to,' she said.

'I'm not mad about it, but Jams has decided we should go ahead and she'll take her chances with Sandra, so I don't have a lot of choice.'

'You wouldn't have quit?' Nick looked shocked. That was two expressions in under a minute. Maybe she was loosening up, or maybe I was just getting better at reading her face.

'Yes, I'd have quit.'

'Because you were scared?'

'Concerned. About her and her baby, and about you.'

'It's soft to worry about other people,' said Nick contemptuously. 'Let them get out of their own messes.'

'Which is why you followed me upstairs and kicked Nappy in the balls?'

'That was different. That was a scam we were pulling together. You don't quit on your mates.'

'OK. Where's Grace?'

'Still at the cottage.'

'Give her a bell, ask her to get on to it, will you?'

'OK.'

'He's very important, you know,' she said as she started to dial.

'Who is?'

'The director person. He's one of the richest men in England. Really big in the City. Hi, Grace.'

I took the receiver to hear a murmur of voices with snatches of song erupting. 'Grace? Alex here. I was going to let Nick talk to you but she tells me Sir Malise Douglas is very important so this is a major-league grovel . . .'

'Hi, Alex. Sorry about the noise, I've got friends staying. Do you want me to ring Malise?'

'Please. I need to find out, urgently, if anyone knew Jacob Stone well when he worked at Catterstone Almack's. Do you think your tycoon could swing it for me? On a Bank Holiday, yet?'

'I'll give it a try. *Sod off!* Sorry, some idiot put an ice-cube down my neck . . . I'll be back to you. Bye.'

She rang off before I could tell her I'd be out until late. Never mind, she'd leave a message.

*

Polly was out for the day with Magnus, looking for houses in Gloucestershire. Dead handy for me: 1) I didn't have to feel guilty about deserting her, 2) I didn't have to see Magnus, 3) I had the use of her car. By one Nick and I were on the motorway heading north, and as far as I could see no one was following us. It would have been easy to spot because the motorway was all-but empty.

We stopped once, for petrol, just past North-ampton, and had a cup of coffee, but that was it. Nick was silent. All the way. A terrific gift, the girl had. I put Mozart on the stereo and I thought. Almost non-stop. For three and a half hours. And by the end I still had no answers, but I'd chewed over everything enough times so I knew exactly what I wanted to find out from Master.

The nearer to Doncaster, the better the weather. The rain was blown away by the wind and the sun was scudding across the flat fields dodging the clouds and making lovely swooping shapes.

Even the drab little streets around the Tubbies sparkled.

The chippy next to Master's was doing a roaring trade. It was the local teenage hangout. Some of them were perched on the low wall in front of the shop, some leaning against the window of the chippy itself, some in the small layby on motorbikes. The bikers were the top of the pecking order, three boys of about seventeen. The rest were much of a muchness except for one girl. She wasn't with the motorbike boys but they wanted to be with her. She was the centre of the group of girls, the queen. Maybe fourteen, fifteen at the most. Small. Slightly chubby. With an astonishing curvy body and kitten-like soft face with a short nose and wide eyes and full pouting lips. She was wearing a tiny cropped tank-top over jeans. Her bare midriff curved seductively, her breasts strained the top, and, even though she wasn't wearing a bra, her breasts thrust forward and up like the figurehead on a plastic surgeon's yacht.

As I parked outside Master's house and Nick and I got out she looked towards us, made a joke, and all the others giggled.

'Shall I sort her out?' said Nick, contemptuous of these Northern hicks.

'Leave it,' I said, and we walked up the path to Master's house.

'I was expecting you, Alex Tanner,' he said. 'Who is this?'

'My assistant, Nick Straker. Nick, this is Abraham Master.'

'You may call me Master. She must wait outside.' He turned and walked back into the house.

'Master?' said Nick. 'Wait outside? What's he on?'

'We'll have to go with it.' I gave her the keys. 'Wait in the car.'

'Can I have expenses for the chippy? I'll get back-ground.'

'Just don't get into a fight,' I said, giving her three quid. Then I followed him down the narrow hall, past

the open door of a room set up as an office with
wooden filing cabinets and on to the kitchen at the
back.

Wonderful set, was my first thought. Perfect thirties. Wooden dresser with plain white china plates,
stone sink, scrubbed wood kitchen table, oil lamp,
wooden chairs, stone flags on the floor, blue and white
checked cotton curtains at the window. China jars
marked Tea and Sugar and Flour, with cork tops. No
plastic bags anywhere. No Harrison Ford either,
though Maggie Whittaker was right, there was an
overtone of Amish.

There was also a strong smell of sweat. No deodor-
ants for Tubbies, presumably. It was recent sweat; he
did wash, but I hoped not to have to stay too long. Or
make him nervous.

He sat at the table and pointed out a chair. 'Be
seated, sister,' he said. 'You ask your questions. I will
answer them, if you have the right to an answer. My
yea is yea and my nay is nay, praise the Lord.'

I sat. He wasn't wearing a suit today, he was in
uniform. Not the cod-Shakespeare kit the pikemen
had worn in the chapel, but a contemporary uniform,
dark blue serge, almost policeman-like, with bright
brass buttons and a brass insignia TT on both sides of
the collar.

'Do you work for a security firm?' I said.

At first I thought he wasn't going to answer. His
wet mouth wobbled around 'No' then settled on, 'Yes.
I run one.'

'You run one?'

'Yes,' he said impatiently. 'TT Express. Owned and run and manned by the church. Can you get to the point, please, I have God's work to do.'

'Fine.' I set the tape recorder running inside my bag. It shouldn't have any trouble picking up his voice: it was deep and projected at me as if I was at the other end of his chapel. 'As I told you, I'm employed to look for Jacob Stone, who seems to have disappeared. My client is a friend, Emily Treliving.'

Master nodded. 'Emily Stone. His wife,' he said. 'That is why I will answer your questions. She has the right.'

'They're married?'

'In God's sight. They exchanged vows.'

'When was this?'

'If you do not know, you should,' he snapped.

I looked at him, trying to get his measure. When I'd first seen him the whole bizarre set-up in the chapel had made me think of him as a freak, not as a person. But if I was going to deal with him now I had to make some assessment of him as a man, otherwise I wouldn't get anywhere.

He was self-important: not surprisingly, since he seemed to be in a position of near-total authority over his sect. He was not, physically, attractive. His balding short fair hair showed a dandruffed scalp, his eyebrows and eyelashes were very fair and made his watery blue eyes look pink, and his wet-lipped face was soft and blobby. But his body was muscular and moved well, and he was sharp enough: the expression in his eyes was confident and aware.

Softly-softly wouldn't do it.

'You mean they were married when they met on the plane? As far as your beliefs are concerned?' I said.

'Of course.'

'Not according to the laws of Britain,' I said. 'Nor of America.'

'The laws of God are greater than the laws of the mumbo-jumbo men.'

'The mumbo-jumbo men?'

'Earthly power.'

'But you enforce the laws of the mumbo-jumbo men, surely? As a security firm?'

'We are the strong arm of the Lord. When he bids us, we fight for the mumbo-jumbo men. We fight in your wars. We serve in your army. I was a sergeant in your army. We fight to the death, and we fight well, to the Lord the glory.'

He paused, probably for a response, and I considered 'Hallelujah!' but rejected it as flippant, and probably un-Tubby. 'How do you know what the Lord wants?'

'He tells the Master.'

'And who is the Master?'

'I am the Master.'

'Who was the Master before you? Your father?'

'No.'

'And if the Lord tells you to fight against the mumbo-jumbo men?'

He gave a short, humourless laugh. 'Don't waste my time, sister. Get on with your questions.'

'When did you last see or hear from Jacob?'

'In early November, last year.'

The most recent sighting. 'And what was he doing in England, from late September to when you last saw him, do you know that?'

'He was preparing to set himself right in the eyes of the Lord.'

'How?'

'You would not understand.'

'Try me.'

'In earthly terms, he was carrying out his mother's last wishes. So he could join his parents with the elect in the Heavenly Kingdom.'

'Join her soon?' I said, jolted. Maybe we had a suicide here.

'In the fullness of the Lord's good time.'

'What was he actually doing, then?'

'He was preparing his presentation to the throne.'

'Master, please explain.'

He expanded, visibly, and his pink neck swelled over his high collar. 'When one of the Lord's anointed passes over to judgement, his name must be numbered in the book of the Lamb, at the throne of the Lord. Only some are elect, and they are numbered. By their birth-name. Our children are not born to us, they are chosen for us.'

'And Jacob didn't know his birth-name?'

'No.'

'Why was that?'

He looked annoyed. 'I was not Master at the time.' Hardly surprising, since he'd only have been seven or thereabouts. 'The Master decided there were special circumstances. So the name was not given to Zeke and Janet Stone, only the means to the name.'

'Which means?'

'I do not know. But I have them, and Emily Stone has the right. And the duty. If Jacob has gone before, unnumbered, she must number him and follow him.'

'You mean she must find his name and take it to the throne?'

'Yes.'

'How soon?'

'There is no time with the Lord.'

Just as well. 'So you'll give me the means?'

'I will give them to you to give to Emily Stone.'

'Why do you have them?'

'Why not?'

'Janet Stone had them, is that right?'

'Yes.'

'And she passed them to Jacob.'

'Yes.'

'And he gave them to you.'

'Yes.'

'Why didn't he keep them? If he was working on it?'

He looked uncomfortable, for the first time. 'He had no more need of them.'

'Why? Because he'd found out?'

'He thought so, yes.'

'Then why give them to you?'

'For safe-keeping.'

'Did he tell you what he'd found?'

'No.'

He could perfectly well have explained to start with, and saved us all this hassle. I looked at him. He looked at me, warily. He'd laid out his ground-rules from the start. Ask, and he would answer. That put the burden on me to find the right questions, and he hoped I wouldn't, because he was hiding something. At the same time his yea had to be yea and his nay, nay.

It made me antsy. With Sandra behind me I was working against time, and I couldn't telephone Master if I had follow-up questions. I'd have to make the time-consuming round trip north.

'Did he think he was in danger?'

'Possibly. Yes.'

'Who from?'

'He did not say.'

'Are you a friend of his? Did he confide in you?'

'We were comrades in the Lord. Confiding was not Jacob's way. It is not our way.'

Pause.

'Could I have the means now, please?'

He opened a dresser drawer, took out a packet and passed it to me. A wave of sweat-smell reached me as he moved, and I put my hand up to my face and smelt my own skin in self-defence. Then I opened the packet.

It was a large folded brown envelope. Inside was a videotape. The printed label said Vari-Vision Video, with a Doncaster telephone number. There was nothing else inside the envelope.

'Do you have a video recorder?' I asked, thinking I knew the answer.

'No. Electricity runs in the veins of the beast.'

'Do you know what is on this tape?'

'The means.'

'Specifically, what the tape shows?'

'Not specifically.'

We looked at each other once more. This was a sensitive spot. I'd shift topics, briefly, and come at him again from another angle.

'Where was Jacob staying in England during late September, October and early November? Up till the time you last saw him?'

'I do not know.'

'When I visited your chapel I saw some children in the congregation. Where did they come from?'

'They are adopted. Plucked by the Lord from the ranks of the beast, and given to the children of light.'

'Which particular beast were they plucked from?'

'There is only one beast, named in the Revelation to John,' he said, looking surprised at my ignorance.

'Where did the children come from?'

'Romania,' he said. 'They are orphans from Romania.'

That made sense, although I wondered how legal the arrangements had been. He didn't seem concerned, however.

'I noticed the chapel was in good repair. That must be expensive. How do your finances work?'

'You do not have the right to an answer.'

'Did Jacob tell you what is in this tape?'

'Hearsay,' he said. 'I will speak only of what I know.'

'You know if he told you. You don't know if what he told you was right. Did he tell you?'

He expelled a breath. 'Yes. He told me.'

'Do you know what happened to Jacob after you saw him last November?'

'I do not know,' he said.

Pause. His breathing was loud in the silence, and the sweat-smell pungent. Maybe my question had been too broad. 'Do you know if Jacob is dead?'

'I do not know.'

There must be a question he was afraid of. I couldn't put my finger on it. To gain time, I said, 'Are you married, Master?'

'I am not,' he said.

'Did Jacob still share your beliefs?'

'This is between a soul and his Lord. Not for me to judge. I do not have the right.'

'But you are the Master.'

'I am the Master of those who choose to follow.'

He was unruffled. The line of questioning was going nowhere. 'The loop,' I said.

He started, like a bad actor registering surprise. His pale blue eyes popped and his mouth dropped open revealing a large wet pink tongue. 'What is your question, sister?'

'What does the loop mean to you?'

He expelled a long, relieved breath.

'You do not have the right,' he said.

Chapter Twenty-Seven

'So the answer's in the video,' Nick said. 'Maybe that's what he meant by the loop. I want a full California Breakfast. Bacon, sausage, hash browns, mushrooms, and two eggs, pancakes with maple syrup and ice-cream, two toast, butter and marmalade, and a cafetiere of coffee. What's a cafetiere? D'you reckon they really eat this lot for breakfast in California?'

It was six o'clock and we were in a café in the first motorway services south of Doncaster. Before heading back to London I'd called on Maggie Whittaker – I'd plenty of questions for her – but there'd been nobody in. I was itching to get home and play the videotape, but we had to eat sometime.

'A cafetiere's a pot with coffee grounds in it. The thing you push down to pour. I've got one.'

'Didn't know the name,' said Nick.

'And I don't think they eat breakfast in California. Just a multi-vitamin high-fibre high-fruit liquid drink before they check their cholesterol level.'

We ordered. Two full California Breakfasts, and I logged it to Jams.

'This is great,' said Nick, looking round at the

family groups crowding the café. 'It's like being away
on a Bank Holiday.'

'It is being away on a Bank Holiday,' I said blankly.

'I mean – not *not* being away. You must know.'

Then I remembered, from my childhood, holidays
were the worst. Christmas and Easter particularly.
The lonely times, when I'd had to pretend to join in
with foster families playing a happy-game whose
rules were beyond me. Or, if I was with my mother
and she'd taken me out, pretending not to notice that
people were looking at her and making out I was
enjoying myself so she wouldn't be disappointed. I'd
just wanted to be alone, then. Alone in my own place.

But for Nick, evidently, it had been different. 'You
wanted to go on trips?'

She nodded. 'Yeah. To an Adventure Park. And
squabble on the way back. That's what the others said
about their trips. You got to eat in cafés and fight on
the way home, in the back seat, with your brother. We
never had a car.'

'Why did you want a brother?'

'When I was little, to take my side at school. You
get lots of stick if you're yellow and slanty-eyed, like
me. I wanted a brother who was a kick-boxer. Great,
here's the food.'

The waitress unloaded her tray until there was no
more room on our table, then she pulled another table
up to take the overspill. Nick started to eat before the
last plate went down.

'Want to know what I found out at the chippy?' she
said when she'd reached the pancakes and slowed up.

'Yes.'

'Northerners are prejudiced.'

'Against half-Asians?'

'Against southerners. They laughed at my accent. I'm not the one with the accent. They are.'

I thought she was making a joke. I don't always know. She helped me out. 'Joke,' she said.

'Ha ha,' I said, waiting for her to come to the point. I knew she had one because she had her cat-smile.

'Guess,' she said.

'Get on with it.'

'Did you notice the one with the tits? Pleased with herself?'

'Sure.'

'How old do you reckon she is?'

'Fifteen?'

'Near enough. Fourteen. How old do you reckon Master is?'

'Thirty-five?'

'Me too. Or older.'

'And?'

'And last year he went to see her parents. To say she was in spiritual danger, and she needed moral instruction, and they should send her along to the church. And then when she was sixteen, he was prepared to marry her.'

'They said no, I suppose.'

'Of course. Don't you think it's funny?'

'Not really.'

'Why not?' She was so taken aback she put down her spoon. 'He's old, and a weirdo. She's—'

'What is she, exactly?'

'A bossy little scrubber. I see what you mean,' she said slowly. 'But nobody would want to marry a Tubby.'

'Some people do.'

'You liked him,' she said accusingly. 'You can't have! All that stuff about names and lists and thrones! He's a crazy, dirty old man! He follows her about, and stares at her!'

'And she doesn't like being stared at?'

'Of course not. It's spooky.'

'Then she shouldn't dress like that. And if he's a dirty old man and she's a bossy little scrubber, what are we?'

'We're normal.'

'OK, if you say so.' I took a pull at myself. It wasn't fair to get at Nick. 'Anyway, it's not that I like him, exactly. It's that I respect him. I trust him.'

'But you said he was hiding something.'

'I trust him to do what he says he'll do. I think he's narrow and smug but I also think he's brave and honest, and not self-indulgent. I think he really believes that what he's doing is right. He'd have married that girl and looked after her, and never touched her, if that's what the rules said.'

'You're losing it,' said Nick, and went on eating.

Maybe I *was* losing it, I thought as I drove the long motorway miles south to London, watching the clouds clot together overhead and the drizzling rain start and the returning holiday traffic build up to a queue. I've never liked narrow people who thought they had all the answers. So what was it about Abraham Master?

I'd envied him, that was it. Just as I envied Jacob Stone without realizing. 'Clear. Directed,' Carl had said. Abraham and Jacob, and Jams come to that, all people with compass needles pointing north, however daft their north might be.

I'd thought I had a north. Security and independence. But my north wasn't far enough away. I'd all but reached it, and what happens to a compass when you're standing at the North Pole?

'Nick? You're good at physics. What happens to a compass at the North Pole?'

She was listening to my tape of the Masters interview. She lifted one headphone clear of her ear and said 'What?'

I repeated it.

'It points to the magnetic north,' she said.

'What if you stand at the magnetic north?'

'Then it points any way you put it. And if you have any sense, you'd point it south. Back to real life where people don't have accents.'

Nine-thirty. I parked Polly's car and we dashed through the wet to my flat. Nick put the coffee on, I went straight for the video, ignoring the flashing light on the answering machine.

'Wait!' said Nick. 'Don't start it till I'm ready. I have to pee.'

'Hurry,' I said, clicking the remote-controls like castanets. I'd been waiting too long for light in the darkness, for some sense out of the mess this case had been from the start.

The toilet flushed and Nick was back. She'd come down the stairs in one leap. 'Right. Go for it,' she said, and I pressed the buttons.

The television flickered and spat. A screenful of nothing. I pressed search, and we watched high-speed nothing for as long as I could bear it.

We were thirty minutes in to a two-hour tape. I passed the remotes to Nick. 'Go all the way through. Every minute,' I said, although I knew what we'd find.

Master had wiped the tape. Or perhaps not Master. But someone had.

Chapter Twenty-Eight

'Nothing,' said Nick, and set the tape to rewind. 'Now what?'

'Fetch the action list. I'll get the answering machine,' I said. I could feel the adrenaline surge. I wouldn't sleep, not for hours.

The first caller was Sandra Balmer. Would I call her please, dear? She'd be available until midnight.

Maybe I would.

The second was Alan Protheroe. Was I sure I was happy with the talking head on the Chicago doco?

I'd already told him, three times, that the talking head was bomb-proof: bright, articulate, well-prepared, high-ranking, good-looking, controversial and black. I fast-forwarded through Alan's witter.

The third caller, Carl Nabokov, sounded miffed. He was real disappointed I'd had to cancel our date. Could I call him?

A meeting for coffee was a date?

Number four. 'Hi, Alex, this is Grace (chuckle). It's about six now. I think you'll be pleased . . . Malise has found you a useful man. He'll be ringing you after seven tonight.'

And there he was, number five. 'Alex Tanner? This is Archie Lawson-Smith from Catterstone Almack's, Monday 7.30. I'll be in all evening. Give me a call about Jacob Stone.' Then he gave an inner London number, which I wrote down.

Number six was Polly. 'Alex, it's just after nine, I'm going out but I've left a message for you on the hall table, can you pick it up yourself and read it, please?'

Polly's message was puzzling – she sounded unusually serious – but she hadn't said it was urgent.

Nick, who'd been listening, said, 'D'you want me to ring the bank man?'

'I will,' I said, and dialled.

He answered on the second ring. I identified myself. 'Hello,' he said, as if I was a friend. 'Good of you to call. Malise wants me to give a hand, if I can, and if Malise says jump, I somersault, don't we all?'

He had a light nasal tenor voice with an upper-class accent and he talked very quickly. I had to strain to catch the words.

'Do you have a pencil?' he went on.

'Yes. Go ahead.'

'The man you want is Jimmy Wood. He left the bank last year but he's the only friend anyone remembers Jacob having. Odd chap, Jacob, do you know him?'

'We've never met.'

'Bloody odd. Anyway, Jimmy liked him, and Jacob rented a room in his flat. Wonderful tenant, I believe. Didn't drink, didn't smoke, paid on time, cleaned like there was no tomorrow. I'll give you Jimmy's address and telephone number.'

I wrote it down. 'Thanks very much,' I said. 'That's exactly what I needed.'

'Don't thank me, tell Malise. Are you really a private detective?'

'Yes.'

'Bloody odd. What's the money like?'

'Oblong bits of security-printed paper with the Queen's head on. Same as yours, I expect.'

He laughed. 'Sorry, was I rude?'

'Not very.'

'Good. Anything else?'

'Not for the moment. I'll get back to you if I can't reach Jimmy Wood.'

'Do that. Bye, PI.'

He rang off.

I dialled. Ring ring. Wood's answering machine. Damn.

I left a ring-back-about-Jacob-Stone message, took the mug of coffee Nick handed me, and sat on the sofa.

'Can I play some music?' said Nick.

'Sure. What?'

'The piano man – that Barty doesn't like. I like him.'

'OK,' I said warily. I hoped Nick wasn't taking sides. The Barty situation was delicate enough without her mixing in.

'Which one?' She held up two CDs.

I didn't want either, much. 'The first piano concerto.'

She put it on and sat down opposite me. 'Action list,' she said, passing it over, with a pen. I started to read it. 'Pun,' she said.

'What?'

'Liszt/list, geddit? What's the matter, Alex?'

I shook my head. I didn't know. Something was hovering around the edges of my mind. Taking sides, that was it. The wrong side. I was looking at something from the wrong side. Or I wasn't looking at something enough, because I didn't want to.

I worked down the list, amending it as I went, and then I looked at what was left.

Abraham Master ?Tubbies' finances ?the loop ?lying
?wiped video
Ring Vari-Vision Video
?Chicago for Eng Lit
?the loop
?Sandra Balmer ?Motive ?Cot and Nappy
Maggie Whittaker
Jimmy Wood
William Alexander – ring/see
ring Carl ?letters

Who or what was I avoiding?

Then it hit me.

Carl, of course. I'd been dodging him because I was embarrassed. I'd thought of him as part of the Barty/me situation, and I didn't want to think of him because of that. And either he or Jams were lying about her letters, and it wasn't her, so it must be him.

Besides, he'd claimed to be keeping Jacob's confidences. Now, with the increasing likelihood of a dead Jacob, I could put pressure on Carl to open up.

'What now?' said Nick. 'What can we do?'

I needed to get rid of her. She was looking at me eagerly like a sheepdog waiting for the whistle and her expectancy made my thought processes freeze up.

The sound of a key in the lock, followed by Barty's entrance, froze them still further. He'd never before let himself in when I was there, without ringing the street doorbell first to warn me. He couldn't have thought I was still out. The curtains weren't drawn and the light from my windows was pouring into the night.

He didn't smile when he saw me, so I didn't either. 'Hi,' I said.

'Hello,' he said. 'Hello, Nick.'

'Hi,' said Nick. 'Alex, d'you want me to fetch Polly's note?'

I'd forgotten it. 'Yeah, do. You know where her keys are.'

Barty stood back to let her pass and then showed me the bottle of wine he was carrying. 'Mind if I open this?' he said. 'It's rather good. Would you like some?'

I read the label. I understood the New Zealand part but the rest was meaningless. 'Should I be impressed?' I said.

'Amused, perhaps. Intrigued. Perhaps even baffled,' he said in a tone I'd never heard him use to me before. Upper-class malicious.

I didn't answer, partly because he was slightly drunk, unusual for him, partly because I felt snubbed, partly because something was clearly the matter, and I didn't know what.

He waited.

'I'd like some, please,' I said cautiously.

He went into the kitchen.

Nick came back and gave me the note. 'What d'you want me to do?' she said.

'What do you have in mind?'

She nodded her head towards the kitchen. 'He wants me out. I can go back to Grace's, unless you want me to stay with Jams. Look after her.'

'No,' I said. Jams had made her own decision about the danger, but I wasn't going to risk Nick. Tough as she thought she was – tough as she actually was – she was still only a kid. 'Go to Grace's. Come over tomorrow morning, eight-thirty.'

'OK,' she said. 'Bye, Barty.'

'Bye,' said Barty, re-emerging with two glasses of wine and giving me one.

I sipped. 'Mmm,' I said. It was white, dry, and tasted faintly of gooseberries. The taste stuck with you for a while after.

I was on the sofa. Barty sat on a chair opposite me and looked at his glass. Cascades of piano notes hung awkwardly in the air between us.

Better not to mention Liszt. He'd stop soon. I read Polly's note.

Alex

Barty came round to pick you up at eight — he seemed to think you and he were having dinner. Were you? He waited in my place. While he was here your Johnny Depp man (it must have been him — tasty American) turned up and rang your doorbell and then mine. Barty wasn't happy. I told the American you were very busy. I think Barty will be coming back tonight, be warned. I'm out with Magnus, be back latish, leave a message on the answerphone if you want a natter.

Love Poll

I couldn't remember if I said I'd have dinner with Barty, but if he thought I had, he was likely to be right.

'Were we supposed to have dinner?' I said.

'Yes.'

'I didn't realize . . . What did I say?'

'After breakfast, I said I'd pick you up at eight unless you cancelled.'

'I'm sorry. Really. I don't think I heard.'

'You never bloody hear,' he said. 'That's because you don't bloody listen.'

'Not now, Barty, all right?'

'Not all right. All wrong. I'm tired of it.'

'Tired of what?'

'Tired of being ignored. Tired of behaving well. Tired of being considerate, and it never being the right time.'

'Is this about Carl?' I said.

'Who's Carl?' he said flatly, and met my eyes.

I was nearly flustered. Mistake, mistake, I thought.

'Carl's the graduate student I met in Chicago. He's turned up in London.'

'Oh, bad luck. You expected him to stay safely in Chicago, filed under "location bonk", I suppose.'

That was so accurate it didn't even hurt when it hit. At least I didn't think it had until I realized my jaw was gaping open. I shut it with an audible click.

Barty went on. 'Of course I'd prefer it if you didn't go to bed with any stray foreigner who asks. But this isn't about Carl. It's about me.'

Silence. We looked at each other.

'You'd better tell me why you're angry, then,' I said. 'Because I honestly don't know.' And I didn't want to hear. Not then and perhaps not ever because it might mean the end of Barty, for me. But it wouldn't be fair to push him away.

He cleared his throat. It was a real danger sign. The last time I heard him do that was two weeks into shooting on location in Uganda, and the next picture showed him being unforgivably insulting to a government official, and the whole crew being deported on the next plane out. He'd written off all the seed money and the research and the footage, and he'd never mentioned it again.

Was I about to be written off?

After the first few weeks, would I mind?

'I've waited for you for years,' he said. 'Patiently. I've put up with your low sexual self-esteem and your penny-pinching and your smugness and your narrowness and your bloody ignorance which you won't remedy—'

'My ignorance?'

'Shut up, Alex. Just shut up for once, and listen. I've even put up with your bloody music and your bloody food, and your habit of parting your legs for any passing dick. You've had your cake with me, and you've eaten it, and you've put some of it into your sodding pension plan. You've never said you loved me. You've known perfectly well that I love you but you never let me say it, and you knew I wanted to marry you, and you wouldn't let me ask.'

'You did ask.'

'Finally. At breakfast, abroad, because I thought you'd feel safer in a public place with a cup of coffee in your hand. Was I wrong?'

I thought about it. 'No,' I said. 'You were probably right.'

'All the compromises are your way. I'm just your sidekick, good enough to use but not good enough to consider. When have you ever asked me what I felt or thought about anything?'

'I asked you what you thought about love at first sight.'

'Because you need to know for a case you were working on. You won't meet my family or my friends, you won't make plans – you won't interrupt your precious work to go away with me – you must have noticed that I invited myself along on the Chicago trip, but you didn't ask why—'

'Why?' I said.

'Because I wanted some time alone with you. Time to talk. But you don't want to talk. You just want the mixture as before. You want to stay in the safe little world you've made for yourself, pretending to be adventurous. You're actually as adventurous as – as – as a *teacake.*'

'A teacake?' I said. For a moment I nearly laughed, then I realized that the unappropriate metaphor was a sign of how upset he was. I was upset too, but I didn't feel it. I felt as if I'd just stepped into a burning bath and knew it was going to hurt, but not yet.

I put down my wine glass and went over to him. I took his glass, put it down, and hugged him. He pulled away and I held on tighter. 'Don't,' I said. 'Barty, don't, I'm sorry. Really. You're probably right, I don't know yet, I'll have to think about it. I'm not very good at relationships, OK? I don't want to lose you. I don't. I don't.'

He pushed me away, so firmly I overbalanced, and got up.

'You can finish the wine,' he said.

And left.

Tuesday, 5 April

Chapter Twenty-Nine

Polly came up just after midnight, and I was glad to see her. I hadn't done anything since Barty left except drink his wine, and I'd never forget the taste. I just hoped I wouldn't always remember it as the taste of a huge mistake.

I couldn't decide whether to go after him or to leave him in peace to get over it. And sober up.

Polly'd brought two bottles of wine and she held them up to me. 'Red or white?'

'I don't care,' I said. 'Anything.'

'You're upset,' she said, when we finally settled down on the sofa. 'You're never upset. Irritated, yes, impatient, yes, but never upset. What is it?'

'Barty. I've made him unhappy. I didn't think I could, not really. And I don't want to.'

'Was it the Johnny Depp man?'

'Only as a symptom. Do you think I'm ignorant, Polly?'

'You? You know more than anyone.'

I'd usually agree with her, I realized guiltily, and that was fundamentally wrong, because nobody knew as much as I thought I knew. Plus if I didn't know

something I said it didn't matter. Which *was* smug.
And narrow.

Barty's judgements are usually generous, but
reliable. Particularly on the people he likes. So if he
criticised me, there'd be truth in it, for sure. And part
of what he said I'd also thought myself. So I felt lowered, diminished. Was I as small as he'd said? I hate
smug people. That's the unforgivable sin, because it
stops you growing.

But most of all I missed him. I wished he'd stayed,
and we could have gone to bed and I'd have hugged
him because that's what I wanted to do. Hug him and
make love to him and make him happy again. If I
could.

Something was itching away at the back of my
mind. Something about making people happy . . .

Polly was talking. 'Are you going to marry him,
Alex? Have you decided? He told me he'd asked you,
when we were talking this evening, it's so romantic he
really loves you—'

'Shut up a second, I'm trying to think—'

Polly subsided, hurt. Not my evening. I stopped
trying to locate my feeling about Barty, and concentrated on Polly, the one I was with. 'Sorry, Poll. I am
upset. I think I've made a mess, and I don't want to.
What did he say to you?'

'All kinds of stuff, but you'll know. About wanting
children soon, and wanting your children, and about
his mother and his grandmother and his childhood
and his dog—'

'His *dog*?'

'Yes, the one who died, and wanting to protect you, and the first time he knew he loved you, and about where you'd want to live and he thought emeralds—'

'Emeralds?'

'Because of your eyes, and Comme des Garçons, and his friend and the production company and I think that's very generous but then he is, and a very good idea and I'm sure you'll make a terrific success of it, and about hinterlands and the meaning of life – why are you making notes?'

'Keep talking,' I said. 'I'm listening.'

'And feeling lonely, and I know exactly what he means about that because I always did at home even though everyone loved me, it's sort of not fitting in, and if everything should be all right then it makes it worse.'

I didn't want to talk about Polly. I wanted to keep listing the things Barty'd told her that he hadn't told me, but that would have been making the same mistake again. I put the pencil down and took a deep breath. 'Is that what you're feeling now?' I said. 'In Hong Kong?'

Polly left at half-past one, happy.

That was something.

I brushed my teeth and combed my hair and put on some of the perfume Barty'd bought me in duty-free. Then I put the list in my jeans pocket and walked up to Notting Hill, to Barty's.

He was still up: the lights were on downstairs.

I let myself in. 'It's Alex,' I called. I could hear music coming from the library. Piano music. Liszt. I walked towards it and opened the door.

Barty was at the piano, with his back to me.

'I didn't know you could play,' I said. 'Liszt's very difficult, isn't he?'

He stopped, but didn't turn round. 'He's very difficult and I'm out of practice.'

'It sounded good, to me.'

'I was cheating. Playing one note in two.'

'It probably improved it. Less sweet. I want to talk to you.'

'What about?'

'A whole load of things.'

'Not tonight.'

'OK. Let's go to bed.'

'Not tonight.'

He didn't sound angry, which was what I'd expected. He sounded tired, and his voice was thick. Why had he never told me he played the piano? Why hadn't I asked? Probably because a piano with piles of old music on it was what I expected in the kind of library he had in the kind of house he had, which wasn't my kind of house. 'Play some more,' I said.

'What shall I play?'

What did he like? I should know. He'd talked to me about music often enough, and I'd only half-listened because he knew so much more than I did and I'd wanted to find out for myself.

He still hadn't turned round.

Somewhere in my head was all he'd ever said to me. I have a good memory. I soak up everything and I don't forget.

'Mozart,' I said.

'Why?'

'Because he's your favourite.'

'Why?'

He was really making me work for it. Fair enough, I supposed. 'Because he makes your soul dance.'

He gave a dismissive click of the tongue. 'Did I really say that?'

'I couldn't invent such a corny line. Come on, play Mozart for me. And do turn round, I'm fed up with talking to your back.'

He faced me. As I'd guessed, he was crying.

'I do love you,' I said.

'Not now,' he said.

Chapter Thirty

We hardly talked at all, after that. He played Mozart for a while and then we went to bed and hugged, and he fell asleep eventually and I lay awake and thought about him and me and what I could do. I slept for an hour or two and woke at dawn. I must have been crying in my sleep. The pillow was wet. Then I went back to sleep until eight, when I got up.

I brought him a cup of coffee before I left and sat on the side of the bed while he drank it. He was polite but uncommunicative.

'Bring me up to date on your case,' he said. I didn't want to. I suppose he thought it a neutral topic, or perhaps he assumed I was preoccupied with it, or perhaps I only ever talked to him about my cases. But the silence had certainly gone on too long, so I did what he asked. 'Any ideas?' I said finally.

'Not really. You'll have plenty of your own.'

'Let's meet later today. Are you working?'

'Thanks for asking. You don't usually.'

'You usually tell me,' I said as gently as I could. 'And I'm glad, because I'm interested, of course.'

'Don't be so bloody considerate,' he snapped, 'it's out of character.'

'Sorry.'

'And don't apologize.'

'Let's have dinner tonight. I'll book, and pay.'

'Where?'

'Alberto's,' I said. It was our most successful compromise: a local Italian restaurant where the cooking was good enough for Barty and the ambience informal enough for me. 'I'll book for eight-thirty. Come round to me about eight.'

'I'm not sure.'

'Please.'

'Very well.'

Back at my flat, Nick was waiting with a cup of coffee and the news that she'd just rung Jams to check she was all right. 'She was fine, no problem.'

'Good.'

'Now what?'

I hadn't given the case one thought since Nick had left the night before, not even when I was telling Barty about it. 'Give me a moment to work it out. Just don't look at me expectantly, it puts me off.'

'Going for croissants,' she said. 'Petty cash?'

I nodded, and she went.

There were no telephone messages. I was pleased to be able to dodge Sandra for a bit longer, but annoyed that Jacob's merchant bank friend hadn't returned my call. He might well be abroad, for months for all I knew.

I tried his number, got the answering machine. Then I rang Archie Lawson-Smith.

He'd clearly been asleep, but when he realised who I was he snapped back on line. 'Good morning, P.I.'

'Good morning, capitalist lackey. I need more help. There's only an answering machine at the number you gave me for Jimmy Wood. Can you track him down? Get a work number, find out if he's away?'

'Sure.'

'Now?'

'Sure. I'll ring you back.'

The next thing on my list was the Doncaster company that had processed the duff video. Chances were they wouldn't open till nine at the earliest, and it was still only ten to, and Nick was out, and I owed Barty an effort . . .

Directory enquiries. William Alexander in Ealing. I was half-surprised he wasn't ex-directory – if I was a headmaster, I would be, to stop enraged parents ringing me at home – but I wrote down the number and dialled it. It was the school holidays, maybe he'd be in.

A woman's voice answered. Middle-aged and slightly whiny. 'The Alexander residence.'

'William Alexander, please.'

'Who wants him?'

A flood of rage came from nowhere. I choked back, 'His daughter' and said mildly, 'Alex Tanner.'

'In connection with what, please?' she persisted.

'From the BBC,' I said. And that was my last effort.

If he couldn't fadge round her with that, then he was not only weak and selfish, but also a slow-witted twit, which was even less forgivable.

'Just a moment,' she said, pleased. Pause. Footsteps. Younger voices in the background. My half-siblings?

'William Alexander speaking.' A pompous, narrow, half-educated, reedy little voice, but perhaps I was prejudiced. 'The BBC, you say?'

'I'm not from the BBC. I'm Susan Tanner's daughter, and yours. Don't put the phone down. The BBC is just cover so you can lie to your wife, so you'd better pretend to be talking to me about something.'

Pause. But he wasn't a complete fool. 'The school's links with industry, you say?'

'Good. This won't take long. I just want the answers to some questions. First, is there any mental illness in your family? Schizophrenia? Alzheimer's?'

'Certainly not.'

'Any other hereditary diseases?'

'Not as far as I'm aware of, no.' Pause. 'Anything else I can help you with?'

This was probably the only time in my life I'd ever speak to my father. What would I wish I'd said?

He spoke again. 'These things aren't always as simple as they appear. Perhaps you could put me more in the picture?'

What did he want to know? If I was going to make trouble for him? Or perhaps simply what I was doing, what I was like?

I imagined his wife listening, eager for her

William to be on the telly. She'd be disappointed. Serve her right. Whatever her life was, it'd be better than my mother's.

'If you give me your number, I could ring back from my office and discuss the matter more conveniently, with all the reference materials to hand,' he said.

An olive branch? Or an opportunity to tell me to piss off without his wife hovering at his elbow?

No point in speculating. Not fair to refuse. I gave him my number, put the phone down, crossed his name off the action list, and wrote *Barty – decide*.

Nick was back. 'D'you want jam, or butter?'

'Both,' I said casually, then heard the words. Barty'd said I wanted to have my cake and eat it. I'd have to watch out for that. If I did try to take from him more than my share, more than was possible, it would hurt us both.

Ouch.

I ate my croissant, enjoying the jam and butter, checked the time, reached for the phone.

'Put it on speaker,' said Nick. I did.

'Vari-Vision Video.' A Yorkshire voice, male, very young.

I told him what I wanted.

'You gorra reference number on the cassette label?'

I gave it to him and heard tap-tap on a keyboard.

'Transfer from Super-8 to VHS, Jacob Stone?'

So the original 'means' had been a film, not a

video. Made sense, since it probably predated Jacob's birth in 1969. 'That's the one.'

'Worrabout it?'

'I'm a private investigator, making inquiries in a missing person case. I'm calling from London. Mind if I ask you some questions?'

'No, you're all right.'

'Did you make the transfer yourself?'

'No, me dad does the old stuff.'

'Could I speak to him? Is he there?'

'I'll gerrim.'

Pause. 'Hello?' Older voice, gravelly, less Yorkshire. Perhaps he'd travelled a bit.

I explained again.

'I know that, me son told me.' He was more cautious, less forthcoming. No point in pulling my punches.

'I think Jacob Stone – the man who brought you the Super-8 – may be dead, and the film may be a clue.'

'You're not police?'

'No. Have you still got the original film?'

'No. I returned it with the VHS cassettes.'

Cassettes, plural. 'How many copies did you make?'

'Two.'

So there was another one somewhere. 'And you checked that the transfer had worked?'

'Yes.'

'So you saw what was on the film?'

'Yes.' He sounded reluctant, almost embarrassed.

'Could you please tell me about it?'

'Mebbe it would be better if you came in to see us.'

'Sorry, I can't get away from London.'

'It's not a very nice thing, over the phone like this.'

'It's really important.'

'How old are you, me duck?'

'Thirty. And very experienced. How old do I need to be?'

He chuckled. 'Thirty'll do for me. You're nothing to do with the police, you say.'

Nick was rolling her eyes in exasperation and making 'get-on-with-it' gestures. I waved to calm her and kept my voice steady. 'Nothing at all. This is just between us.'

'It's a grey area, see, and I don't want any bother.'

'There'll be no bother from me.'

'Oh, well then – it was a loop, wasn't it?'

'Yeah!' said Nick.

'A loop?' I said encouragingly.

'You wouldn't know about loops, being a lass of your age, see, but I've been in the film industry all me life and down south in the late Sixties, and truth be told I shot some of them. Ten minuters, Super-8 porno jobs, semi-amateur performers, professional crew.'

'Ten-minuters?'

'To be shown in booths, in sex shops, like. Ten minutes being—' he stumbled—

'A satisfactory length of time? For the purpose?' I looked firmly away from Nick, who was making crotch-rubbing gestures and mouthing 'Design fault'.

'You gorrit,' he said, relieved.

'Did you recognise any of the talent?' I said, using the TV word for performers, trying for rapport.

It worked. His voice warmed and relaxed even more.

'Worked in TV, have you?'

'Done a bit. You're a cameraman, then?' I said respectfully. Cameramen are the technical aristocrats.

'Was. Got me own business now. Gives me more time with the family, and all. But I miss it. Yeah, I miss it. Oh, well, about the talent – no familiar faces. But there wouldn't be, mostly, with the loops.'

'Any credits?'

'No crew-credits, of course. Three performers, two women and a man. Sexy Sandra, Sweet Sally and Big Dick Tracy. Directed by Keeper Hardon.'

I laughed. So did he.

'I've got one of your cassettes here,' I said. 'But it's been wiped.'

'None of my doing. They both left here orright.'

The call-waiting bleep went. I signed off from the Doncaster call quickly but gratefully, making sure I could get back to him, and took the new one. It was Archie Lawson-Smith. 'Hi, P.I. Jimmy Wood's at their Singapore branch for a month, it's eight hours ahead, they tell me he's still at his desk, here's the number.'

I took it. 'Thanks very much, Archie.'

'Don't thank me. Just tell Malise.'

I put the phone down.

'We've got the loop,' said Nick, delighted.

'We've *identified* the loop. We still haven't *got* it,' I said.

'Bet you Sexy Sandra is Sandra Balmer.'

'I'm sure you're right. But who's Sweet Sally?'

'And Big Dick Tracy and Keeper Hardon.'

'I'm not so bothered about them . . . I'll try Jimmy Wood in a minute. I've got to work out the right questions to ask him, first.'

'You sound disappointed. You should be pleased. What's the matter?' said Nick.

'Don't know,' I said. 'I expected the loop to be something else, I suppose. Something more significant.'

Nick clicked her tongue impatiently. 'It's been significant enough for Jacob, I reckon,' she said.

Chapter Thirty-One

Jimmy Wood was at his desk, and we had one of those clear long-distance lines, better than a local call, that make you forget the thousands of miles between.

He was very different from Archie Lawson-Smith. I should have expected that, since he was a friend of Jacob's, and I couldn't imagine the Jacob I knew having much time for Lawson-Smith, who sounded like Prince Charles on speed.

Wood's voice was deeper, much slower, and there was a perceptible thought-pause before every answer.

When I finally put him in the picture, there was a very long pause indeed. Then he said, 'I am extremely sorry to hear it. Jacob feared as much.'

'As much? What do you think's happened to him?'

Pause. 'Something unfortunate, clearly. I am very sorry.'

Pause. 'I hope not,' I said, to prompt him.

'It must have. Otherwise he would have been in touch with me. And with Emily Treliving.'

'He told you about her?'

Pause. 'Yes.' Pause. 'I must speak directly to her, before I pursue this matter with you.'

'She's very upset.'

'Understandably. I would try not to upset her further.'

'I'm her agent.'

'I need to hear that from her.'

He wouldn't be budged. I rang off, rang Jams, soothed her, gave her Wood's number, and waited for his return call, jittering about, dusting. Nick watched me impassively.

As the minutes stretched into the quarter-hour, she said 'What is it now?'

'Sandra,' I said. 'We've had nothing from Sandra for a while. I don't trust her, and it's making me itchy. I want to get the loop sorted and get back to her, actually knowing what I'm talking about.'

'You can always vacuum,' suggested Nick. Unhelpfully.

I did.

I didn't catch the phone over the hoover noise. Nick heard, answered and put it on speaker.

'Jimmy Wood here.'

'Alex Tanner. Just a moment.' I scribbled down the questions I needed to ask. 'OK, go ahead.'

'Jacob left a package in my keeping, for Emily Treliving, or for return to him, if he asked for it. I've now checked with Emily that she wants it handed over to you, so it's ready for you to pick up at my office.' He gave me a name and address of a bank in the City. 'Go to Reception, ask for Peter Quill, and produce some identification, preferably a passport and a business card. Clear?'

'Very clear. Very directed.'

'What?'

'Never mind. Do you know what's in the package?'

'Yes. A video cassette and a letter for Emily.'

'Have you seen the video?'

'No.'

'When did Jacob give it to you?'

'In early November last year. He'd been staying at my flat, and he gave it to me when he left for the States.'

'Was he going directly to the airport?'

'No. He had a meeting first.'

'Who with?'

'I have no idea.'

'What did he say to you about what he was doing?'

'That he was sorting out some matters in connection with his mother's estate.'

'And as far as you know he intended to go back to Chicago, to his graduate work?'

'Absolutely. He was enjoying it, and looking forward to his career and his marriage. I wish—' His voice tailed off.

'So do I,' I said. 'But it's not likely he's all right, is it? He's not the sort of person who would change his plans without notifying the university, for instance.'

'Quite.' Pause. 'Anything else I can help you with?'

'Tell me what you know about the videotape.'

'What?'

'Everything.'

'Well . . . he called me towards the end of September, last year. He came to my flat to watch the tape, as he had no other access to a video machine. He asked to watch it alone. He watched it for a few minutes, then joined me in the kitchen. He didn't comment, but he seemed . . .'

Pause.

'What did he seem?'

'Very hard to describe. Jacob was reticent. Self-contained. Is it important?'

'Could be, very.'

'Well then.' Pause. 'He seemed – illuminated. As if he had the solution to a puzzle. And also, slightly, amused. Not laughing amused. More like sardonic.'

'Cynical?'

'Not exactly. Satisfied, a bit superior. Mind you he was arrogant, always.'

'What next?' said Nick, after Wood rang off.

'What do you think?'

'You go and fetch the package. With your passport and all. What'll I do?'

I told her.

As I'd expected, Jacob's letter to Jams was virtually useless to me, especially as she wouldn't let me read it. It was very useful to her, though. She read it again and again, tears trickling down her pudding face. 'He really loved me,' she said eventually, sipping the camomile tea I'd made for her when I'd finally stopped trying to read his tiny writing upside-down. 'I knew it. We knew it. We felt the hand of God touch us.'

I didn't say – I tried not to even think – that the

hand of God should have kept its eye on the ball and followed through to deliver Jacob safe.

I looked at the sealed envelope containing the video tape, sitting demurely on the beautifully polished little table in the little house that had been so lovingly chosen for a man who had never seen it. I looked out at the twee window-boxes, where the sweetpeas trembled in the breeze and drank in the light drizzle. 'D'you want me to finish the job?' I said.

'Oh, yes. He says I can use the tape if I want, to get the name of his mother. Because of his faith—'

'To take to the throne of the Lord?'

'You know about that?'

'Abraham Master told me.'

'But Jacob says it would be better if I didn't watch the tape myself.'

'Because it's pornographic?'

'He just says, not suitable. And he doesn't want me involved. He says I should ask Jimmy Wood. But he's in Singapore, isn't he? Should I wait for him to come back?'

'We can't afford to wait.'

'OK, you do it, Alex? And then just give me the name, nothing else?'

'Sure. Can I make a telephone call?'

'Of course.'

I rang Nick. 'Everybody's here. More than everybody. Sort of waiting,' she said uneasily. She didn't like social situations.

'Good. Make them all coffee, get some biscuits.'

'We're out of coffee. No money in petty cash.'

'Borrow from – Barty.'

'OK. How long will you be?'

'Twenty minutes. Hang in there.'

Jams was still reading the letter with the air of one who would be reading it many more times until she died, which could be sixty years. If I did my job properly.

She rubbed her baby-bump as she read.

'Are you sure there's nothing to help me in there?' I said.

She looked up dreamily. 'Nothing at all. Apart from the bit about his mother's name, it's all about us.'

'No mention of anyone else? Or anything that he's done, or going to do?'

'No, I've told you,' she said, sounding as near to cross as I've ever heard her.

'Do you still want me to go on with this?'

'Do you think I should?'

'I think the more we know the safer you'll be.'

'Up to you. Decide for me. Please, can I be alone?'

Chapter Thirty-Two

My flat isn't designed for entertaining more than three people. It was well overcrowded when I got back with the video cassette: Nick had done all I'd asked her, and more.

I'd guessed that Jacob's letter wouldn't give me his mother's name and I'd have to use the tape. From what Jimmy Wood'd said, I knew Jacob had identified her in minutes.

It could just have been because she was very famous, and so I'd know her immediately. But time was pressing and I wouldn't count on it. So I wanted people from Jacob's worlds: Doncaster, Oxford and London merchant banks. There was nothing I could do, at such short notice, about Doncaster, although if I drew a blank with this audience I'd take the tape up north to Maggie Whittaker and Master, if I could get him near a machine. For Oxford, I had Grace Macarthy. For the City, Archie Lawson-Smith. For general knowledge and a good eye, Barty.

Those three were there. But so was Polly, who'd dropped in to see me and wanted to join in, and Magnus, who'd come to pick her up.

The sofa and chairs had been re-arranged in a semi-circle round the television and the group were drinking coffee out of ill-assorted mugs, eating short-bread and chatting. They seemed to be enjoying themselves. Archie Lawson-Smith was about my age, tall and thin, with receding slicked-back blond hair, a long narrow nose and pale-blue quick eyes. He was the most formally dressed, in an expensive, rather sharp dark suit, lightly striped shirt and bright Italian designer tie.

He and Magnus had obviously hit it off and were talking derivatives, with Polly listening politely.

Grace had probably come straight from bed. Her slightly frizzy dyed brown hair was piled casually on top of her head, and she was wearing a long shapeless black t-shirt over black leggings. She looked content-edly forty-five, and experienced, and amused. She nearly always looked amused.

No sign of Nick. I assumed she was in the kitchen, hiding.

I said 'Hi!' to my coffee-klatsch, smiled at Barty who half-smiled back and went right on talking to Grace, picked up some paper from the desk and went straight through to Nick. 'Well done,' I said.

'Magnus knows banking too,' said Nick. 'Pompous git, but he could be useful.'

'Could be. Come on, let's get this show on the road.'

'Too many people,' she said.

'Never mind,' I said tearing the paper into strips.

'Give them one of these and a pencil each. And take one yourself.'

I put the tape in the video machine and turned to face the audience, who were now clutching paper and pencils. I felt like Poirot in the last scene of a lumbering Christie film.

'What you're going to watch is a very short pornographic film from the late sixties. I need to know if you recognize any of the performers. There are three: Sexy Sandra, Sweet Sally and Big Dick Tracy. If you think you know anyone, please write their names down. Don't say them, I don't want you influencing each other. Remember this was over twenty-five years ago.'

'Can we give them marks out of ten?' said Magnus.

Polly smiled. Grace didn't. I got the impression she'd taken an immediate dislike to Magnus, who she was sharing the sofa with. 'Whatever you like,' I said, and started the tape.

My Doncaster ex-cameraman had done a good, clean transfer and the original film techs must have been good. The lighting was flattering, the sound sharp, and the cameraman used five angles.

There the professionalism ended. The set was somebody's bedroom and the script was dire.

Not as bad as the performers, however. Sandra Balmer was easily the best and she was as wooden as a chest of drawers. The film opened with her lying on the bed, fully dressed. 'Oh, it's hot in here,' she said to no one in particular. 'I'll make myself more comfortable.' She undressed, slowly, down to a push-up pink bra, pink frilly knickers, a white suspender-belt and white stockings. 'I feel really hot,' she said, rubbing her bouncy breasts.

The door opened and an adolescent girl came in. Sixteen at the most, and out of her head on downers, judging by her dead eyes. She was lovely, film-star lovely, with thick dark hair, a small nose, full promising lips and slender well-shaped limbs. She was in a very short school uniform, with black stockings and visible black suspenders. 'Oh! Auntie Sandra! What are you doing! That's naughty!' she said, with all the emotion of British Rail announcing a train delay due to leaves on the line. She had a thin, well-brought-up little voice.

'Hello, Sally, dear, back from school already, isn't it hot, let's be naughty together,' said Sandra, robustly Yorkshire.

Then they were naughty together, for a bit.

So far only one of my audience had written anything.

Grace. And she wasn't smiling as she wrote, so she didn't find it funny.

On the screen, Sandra and Sally had run out of naughty and looked as if they were waiting for an interruption.

No retakes, sloppy cutting.

The camera-angle shifted to the door.

A man, thirtyish, tall, in tight white shorts and a blue sweater, carrying a tool-bag.

There was a flurry of writing from my audience.

Grace. Barty. Magnus, Polly. Lawson-Smith, who'd gone pale. And, surprisingly, Nick.

'I'm Richard Tracy. They call me Big Dick,' said the man on the screen. The camera focus-pulled to a close-up of his crotch. Either it was augmented with clingfilm or they were right. 'I'm the plumber. I hear you're having trouble with your plumbing.'

He was no plumber. He was posh. He was no actor either, but he was enjoying himself, and he said his lines with an amateur's pride in having learnt them and in delivering them loudly. 'Oh, you saucy girls, what are you up to?'

The girls weren't up to anything; they were lying side by side like stockinged fish on a slab. The cameraman cut to a low angle, up Sally's bum, which was as delicious as the rest of her. I glanced at Barty, who was watching impassively. I didn't know if he liked porn. All men did, probably. Did he like Sally?

'Seen enough?' I said, pausing it.

'Yes,' said Lawson-Smith. 'I have to get back to the office.'

'Let it run, come on,' said Magnus.

I let it run and showed Lawson-Smith out. 'Are you going to give me your piece of paper?' I said, when we reached the street-door.

'You won't need it,' he said.

'Please?'

He folded it tightly and gave it to me.

'Thank you very much,' I said. 'You've been terrific.'

'Don't thank me. Just don't tell Malise,' he said.

I opened his piece of paper as he hurried away. One line of writing. *Big Dick Tracy: Malise Douglas*, it read.

I stood in the hall, and thought. That could be the money, then, and the power, behind Sandra and Brownlow. Big Dick Douglas. Jacob's father?

I needed Grace's piece of paper, badly. She was the only one who seemed to have got Sweet Sally.

I went up the stairs, two at a time.

The film had finished: Nick was running it back.

'Not bad at all,' said Magnus. 'Ten out of ten for Sweet Sally,' and he made a locker-room 'wer-wer' noise. Polly looked slightly miffed; Grace made a dismissive face and folded her paper as tightly as Lawson-Smith had. 'For your eyes only, Alex,' she said. 'We must talk about it.'

'OK,' I said, collecting hers and then the rest. 'Thanks very much, everyone.'

'We'd best be off,' said Magnus. 'Things to do, houses to see, eh, Polly?' He took her elbow possessively.

Polly smiled.

'I assume you want us to keep quiet about this,' Magnus said to me. 'You have my word on that.'

'Thank you,' I said.

They left, and the atmosphere relaxed several notches.

'Frightful man,' said Grace.

'Yuck,' said Nick. 'I don't know why he pretends not to be gay.'

'Gay?' I said. It was unexpected but not surprising. 'Why do you think so?'

'You weren't here for the rest of the film,' said Barty.

'And?'

'Guess what he looked at?' said Nick. 'The whole time?'

Barty and Grace were nodding.

'The design fault?' I said.

'The big design fault,' said Nick.

'D'you want me out?' said Barty, getting up.

'Not for me,' said Grace.

'No, please stay,' I said, as eagerly as I meant but more eagerly than I had meant to sound. I was reading the pieces of paper. Everyone except Nick had written *Malise Douglas* for Tracy. Nick had written *a punter who likes corsets*, presumably information gleaned from her mother's friends working the streets of Paddington.

Grace had also written: *Sweet Sally – Lady Douglas, née Sally Newcomb*.

'Ah,' I said, looking at her.

'Ah indeed.'

'Council of war?' she said. 'I need to be put in the picture first.'

'Nick can do that,' I said. 'I'm going to have a bath.'

Chapter Thirty-Three

I always enjoy a bath, but this one was a device to be alone and decide exactly what I thought about the case and what I wanted to do before discussing it with a heavy roller like Grace.

It took ten minutes and even then I wasn't sure I'd covered all the bases, but I didn't think more time would help. I'd got to the stage where what I needed was the information that only she could give.

So I dressed and went downstairs.

'Sorted it out?' said Barty. Not sneering: affectionate.

I smiled at him. I did love him, really I did, if love was liking plus desire. But what if it was more, and I'd missed it so far?

'Come on,' said Grace impatiently. 'What are you going to do next?'

'Listen to you telling me about Sir Malise and Lady Douglas.'

'What do you know about him?'

'Nothing at all, other than what Nick told me you'd told her, and what I saw in the loop. He's very rich, and powerful in the City. He's vain. He likes sex. That's it.'

'Right. There isn't much more, except he's very bright and a good friend of mine.'

'And a lover,' said Barty.

'Oh, well, that's nothing special. His little black book would fill a CD-rom. Apart from casual affairs and one-nighters—'

'—and working girls,' interjected Nick contemptuously.

'—he has three households. With his wife Sally in Buckinghamshire. With Marie-Louise and two children near Nice. With Campanita and three children near Seville.'

'Sally has no children?'

'Not unless Jacob was hers.'

'What's Sally like?'

'Beautiful to look at, as you saw. Very fragile. Has nervous breakdowns all the time. Doesn't go out much. Spends all her energies on the garden.'

'Where is she treated?'

'I'm not sure, but when Nick told me about Brownlow, I wondered, too. He's exactly the kind of shrink Malise'd choose, and the Caritas the kind of clinic. Very discreet.'

'What's their relationship like?'

'Malise loves her. Best, I think. But he's not a man to devote himself destructively to a batty wife and he's got a thing about children, and he always told me she couldn't have any. I've often thought that he kept two

other families rather than one so that she'd be less
jealous.'

'She knows about them, then?'

'Oh, yes. Everybody does. But she knows how
much he loves her.'

Brief silence.

'So what does it mean?' said Nick impatiently.
'And what shall we do?'

'Hang on a minute, Nick,' I said. 'Grace, do you
think Malise'd mind if that loop was common knowledge? If it was splashed over the tabloids, for
instance?'

'He wouldn't care at all for himself; he's a reckless
exhibitionist, he comes out of it rather well, and it's
very long ago. For Sally – not so easy to tell, but she's
well protected, and she's never photographed so most
people wouldn't recognize her anyway. The estate's
crawling with security, she doesn't read the papers,
she's cocooned. She has a very small circle of
friends . . . I've only met her once, when her gardens
were open to the public.'

'I didn't know you liked gardens, Grace,' said Nick.

'I don't, much, but I wanted a butcher's at Sally.'

'Why?' I said.

Barty smiled.

Grace looked awkward. Unusually. Breezy and
complete disclosure was her normal mode. 'Total confidence?'

'Of course,' I said.

'Nick?'

'I swear,' said Nick.

'Barty knows already . . . We're talking ten years ago. I was thirty-five.' She ground to a halt.

'And Malise thought you'd be a great head to a fourth household?' I said, to help her out.

'I'd lost my nerve. Briefly. About the future. I wanted more children. Then I looked at Sally, and I couldn't.'

'You actually considered being part of a *harem*?' said Nick, deeply shocked, her heroine wobbling. 'But you told me, women should make their own lives. You told me.'

'Wait till you're older, Nick,' I said. I'd never felt warmer towards Grace, and I showed it by not showing it and ploughing straight on. 'How do you think Malise would feel about Sally having a child?'

'It would depend if it was his. But if it was, why would she have given it away? Doesn't make sense. He's always been very dynastic. And generous. He can afford to be. Each of his kids gets a well-funded childhood and a million in cash when they turn eighteen,' said Grace.

'A million,' I said, wheels clicking inside my head. 'When did he marry Sally?'

'1971,' said Barty. 'I was at the wedding. With Miranda.'

'Who's Miranda?' said Nick.

'His *first* wife,' said Grace, looking at me.

'You straights are hopeless,' said Nick. 'So messy. I'll love you for ever, oops, no I won't, how can you trust each other?'

I ignored her. I'd reassure her later. 'So Jacob was

born before their marriage. When Sally was very young, and stoned most of the time, probably . . . Thanks, Grace, you've been a great help.'

'A million's a lot of money,' said Barty lightly. 'You will be careful, Alex?'

'Very,' I said. 'Very. And I'll meet you at Alberto's at eight. Have you booked, Nick?'

'Table for two, eight o'clock, upstairs,' said Nick.

'Grace, one more thing,' I said. 'Your chap in Aberdeen. The authority on sects. Can I have his number?'

'We've got it already,' said Nick. 'In my notes.'

'Why?' said Grace.

I shook my head. 'Not important,' I said.

'OK, then. What time is it now?' said Grace.

'Just after twelve,' said Nick.

'Take me to lunch, Barty,' said Grace, chuckling. 'Perhaps not to Alberto's.'

When we were alone, Nick looked at me uncomfortably. 'Alex . . .'

'Yes?'

'What do you think they're going to do?'

'Have lunch,' I said firmly.

'But when Grace chuckles like that . . . I don't like that bit of her.'

'Nick, it's a waste of time being jealous of Grace. She's just herself. She's not your lover anyway, is she?'

'How do you know?' said Nick aggressively. 'She might be.'

Silence.

'Anyway, Barty's your lover,' she said. 'Isn't he? Don't you care what he does?'

'It's just loops, Nick. What people do. Because it's familiar, and comforting, and they can stay on the rails that way. Grace's confidence was shaken by remembering how nearly she signed up with Macho Malise. Grace's confidence is an awesome thing, so the shaking of it is that much worse. Barty'll comfort her.'

'Don't you care about him?'

'Of course. But he's feeling threatened too, and irritated with me, and he and Grace go back a long way, and I'm sure she's good value. Besides, he's been watching porn.'

'*That*?!' said Nick. 'He *can't* have liked that . . . I don't understand.'

'Just a guess.'

Silence.

'So what do *we* do?' said Nick bleakly.

'We have our own loop.'

'Which is?'

'Guess.'

She pushed up her cap and tugged at her hair anxiously. Then she smiled. 'Work,' she said.

'You got it.'

Chapter Thirty-Four

The voice of Professor Fairlie, Grace's sect man, squeaked through the phone speaker at Nick and me. He sounded educated, Scots, old and entirely unsurprised by my call. He brushed aside my introduction. 'If you need to know about the Tubbies, I'll tell you what I can, but I'll ask you to make it short, since lunch-time approaches.'

'Very few questions,' I said.

'Fire away.'

'It looks to me as if the Tubbies got an injection of money a few years ago. Their church is in very good repair. Any idea what that came from?'

'The sale of the Thomas Tubmaster collection to Chicago University in 1989, I would think.'

'The collection?'

'Tubmaster's books and a great deal of manuscript material, owned and preserved by the sect. I was surprised they decided to sell, but they had a forward-looking Master at the time and the collection fetched a substantial sum.'

'That wasn't the current Master, Abraham, was it?'

'No. Abraham took over some two years ago.'

I crossed *?Tubbies finances* off my list.

'Most of the male Tubbies go into the Army for a short time, is that right?'

'All the male Tubbies go into the Army. It is their duty to prepare to fight for the faith.'

But Jacob didn't. 'So if one doesn't, why would that be?'

'Your guess is as good as mine. Perhaps the Army wouldn't accept him on health grounds? If he stayed within the sect, that is the only reason that comes to mind.'

'Perhaps,' I said. But Jacob had seemed healthy, and he hadn't told Jams he wasn't.

'They are, as you've probably gathered, heavily militaristic. The Tubbies lost a whole generation in Flanders in the 14–18 war. Courage, endurance and heroic self-sacrifice are key Tubby virtues.'

The First World War. In Flanders fields . . . The tips of my fingers itched and the tumblers in my mind were clicking round into line like a fruit machine. Then they stopped clicking, and I saw it. Not a line of fruit. A line of flowers. And a face.

Nick saw my expression. 'What is it? Alex, what is it?'

'Early November,' I said.

'What?' said Nick.

'Miss Tanner? Are you there?' said Fairlie impatiently.

Very nearly there, I thought. Almost. Then I concentrated again. 'Something completely different,' I said. 'Are Tubbies required to give a certain proportion of their income to the church?'

'Indeed. Fifty-one per cent goes to the Lord, in the form of the current Master.'

'Fifty-one per cent . . . Would that also apply to a large one-off payment?'

'It applies to any money received. Money is the currency of the beast.'

'Last question,' I said. 'The Tubbies are opposed to modern inventions, I understand. They're forbidden the use of electricity, for instance.'

'Exactly so.'

'How do they cope in the Army? With modern communications equipment? Most of that must be electricity-based.'

'They are permitted to use what they must.'

'And now they run a security firm. They must use electricity in that, and videos for surveillance, surely?'

'The same would apply. They use the tools of the beast for the work of the Lord.'

'Thank you, Professor,' I said. 'Enjoy your lunch.'

When he'd rung off, Nick said, 'I don't understand.'

'Neither do I, completely,' I said.

Then I dialled Sandra.

'My dear! I'd almost given you up! But I expect you were *very busy*,' she said.

'I was. I've got the loop, and I know who Jacob's father was.'

Silence. 'Aren't you clever?' she said. 'Have you told dear Jams?'

'We need to talk. Not on the telephone. Urgently,' I

said. 'Can you take a train down this afternoon? That'd be much quicker.'

'I *could . . .*' she said consideringly.

'And bring Abraham Master with you. The head of the Tubbies, you know—'

'Yes, I know who you mean. That might be difficult . . .'

'Tell him I have the right. Then he'll come. And I want Cot and Nappy there, as well.'

'Cot and Nappy?'

'Your two hard men who were staying at Balmer Leisure Services. The ones you told about me.'

'Derek and Dennis?'

'If they're the ones who look like wrestlers. I want them with us when we have our chat.'

'Will you be bringing any chums?' she fished. 'It'll be a friendly little chat, I hope?'

'To our mutual advantage. I don't want to make trouble. I just want to tie up the case for my client. I'll bring my assistant, Nick.'

'Such a sweet girl, I'll look forward to seeing her again,' she said warmly. Nick made a vomit-face while Sandra gushed on. 'Shall we say – six o'clock? At my little place in Queen's Park? We'll be very comfy there, and I'm sure you can find it again, after dropping in unannounced the other morning.'

'I'm sorry about that,' I said insincerely.

'I was disappointed you didn't trust me, but I understood, a girl has to look after herself, doesn't she?'

'OK, see you in Queen's Park at six. And – one

291

more thing – I might bring an American friend. A man.'

'A man?'

'A friend of Jacob's.'

Pause. 'Will he be – difficult?' she said.

'Absolutely not. Very co-operative, I'm sure,' I said. 'We'll all be chums together.'

'So long as you're certain,' she said. 'I do hate awkwardness, don't you?'

We rang off at the same time.

'Now what?' said Nick.

'Now we make the date with Carl,' I said. 'And then there's something I want you to get for me.'

Chapter Thirty-Five

I'd asked Carl to meet us at my flat at half-past five. He was early, and eager. Less so when he saw Nick. He looked to me just as beautiful as he had in Chicago – much more beautiful than Johnny Depp – but more foreign. His race-cocktail skin bloomed exotically in the blurred, muted London light. It was drizzling outside and his face, dewy from the damp, reminded me of a rain-forest flower in the tropical house at Kew Gardens.

As I settled him down on the sofa and Nick made him a cup of coffee, I wondered at myself. How had I ever had the chutzpah to sleep with a man so obviously not just rungs but whole ladders above me in the sexual pecking-order? Why had I not smelt Hamelins-full of rats?

Perhaps I had. And sprayed the smell away with aerosols full of rationalization.

'I'm real glad we've managed to meet up,' he said, quickly and quietly, before Nick came back. 'I've been thinking about you, ever since . . .' He left the rest of the sentence for his eyes to finish. 'We can spend some more time together? Alone?'

'Possibly tonight,' I said. 'As I told you on the phone, I need you to help me out at a business meeting first. As a friend of Jacob's.'

'I don't see how that can be,' he said. 'I don't see what help I can give.'

I smiled.

'Black, no sugar,' said Nick, thrusting a mug at him.

He smiled at her captivatingly. She stared back, uncaptivated. 'So who's involved in the business meeting?' he said, clearing his throat.

The front door of Balmer Leisure Services was opened by a dyed blonde, motherly woman in her early forties wearing a nanny's uniform and smelling strongly of baby powder. 'You must be the visitors for Sandra,' she said. 'She wants a word with Alex alone first. If you two nice people wait in here, I'll bring you a big mug of cocoa.' She opened one of the doors on the right of the hall.

'That OK with you, Alex?' said Nick.

'Fine with me,' I said. 'You can keep Carl company. In you go, both of you.'

'It's a normal office,' said Nick, surprised. I don't know what she'd been expecting: desks in the shape of baby-changing tables, perhaps.

But she was right, Balmer Leisure Services had a perfectly normal office, about twelve feet square, with a large desk, several chairs, and filing cabinets. I stuck my head in to check there was no sign of Master or

Cot and Nappy. I didn't want them getting together yet.

'It's Nick and . . .?' said Nanny.

'Carl,' I said.

'Nick and Carl. For the mugs,' she said obscurely, then led me two doors further, knocked and ushered me in.

It was a small room, furnished like a sitting-room with a real coal fire surrounded by a large fender over which children's vests and pants were draped to air, two armchairs, and a large, open, wooden sewing-box on legs. Visible in the sewing-box was knitting-in-progress, a few lines of soft blue wool on narrow needles. On the mantelpiece was an array of photographs of small children, in silver frames. Sandra was sitting in one of the chairs. She was wearing cream trousers, a pink silk shirt, a cream cashmere cardigan, and big shiny pearls around her neck and in her ears. There was a pile of small grey woollen socks in her lap.

'Alex! How lovely! Just sorting the socks for darning,' she said. 'Very important not to get behind with the darning. Waste not, want not. The young nannies don't really understand, do they? As soon as a potato appears in a little one's dear little sock, they throw it away and buy another pair. Not in Nanny Sandra's nursery, oh no. Do you know what a potato is, dear? It's what we used to call a hole . . .'

'Cut the crap, Sandra,' I said briskly. Anxiety was making her drivel. 'Are they all here? Master, and Cot and Nappy?'

'Do sit down,' she said sharply, all the warmth

gone from her voice. 'Don't tower over me like that . . .'

When you're five foot and a bit you don't often get accused of towering. Rather pleased, I sat down in the other chair.

'They're here,' she said. 'In other rooms. Abraham demanded a room to himself for his evening devotions. He's such a . . .' her voice died, and all I could hear was the gentle hissing of the fire. The room must be sound-proof. All the better.

'Right,' I said. 'I'll tell you what I think I know, OK, and then we sort out what to do.'

'You're so direct and commanding,' she said. 'And you have such a full bust. Ever thought of taking up my line of work?'

I disregarded her. 'I've told nobody what I'm going to tell you,' I said. 'Except Nick. And most of it need go no further, as far as I'm concerned, though I will tell Jams what happened to Jacob.'

'Do you think she'll make trouble?'

'No,' I said. 'I think I can promise you that.'

'Get on with it,' she said, sounding more Yorkshire. Her hands were shaking.

'Jacob is the child of Sally, now Douglas, and Malise Douglas, born before they were married. Right?'

'Right.'

'Sally was a dim, well-brought up child who somehow got involved in drugs and porn in the late sixties.'

'She was unhappy at home,' said Sandra.

'And you took care of her, didn't you? And so when

296

she got pregnant, she came to you, and you looked after her?'

'Yes.' She rubbed her hands together in her lap. 'It was a terrible thing for Sally. She was a child herself, and very vulnerable, and we had no idea that Malise was serious . . .'

'So she didn't tell Malise, and she had the baby, and you gave it to your sister to bring up. Then I suppose Malise reappeared on the scene and they married . . .'

'He really loves her,' she said. 'He's always looked after her.'

'And she couldn't have any more children.'

'Jacob's was a very difficult birth.'

'When did she tell Malise about Jacob?'

'Not until Susan died.'

'Didn't she ever think of taking Jacob back, to bring up herself, with Malise?'

Sandra shook her head. 'Sally didn't think it would be fair to Jacob. To take him away from the home he knew . . .'

'OK,' I said. 'But after Susan died, Jacob had the means. To trace his mother. And he didn't recognize her from the loop but he recognized Malise, and he came to you to tell you what he knew because Susan'd told him that you'd made the arrangements for his adoption.'

'You're a clever girl,' she said shakily.

'And you knew that Malise gives all his children a million when they turn eighteen, and Jacob was past due for payment. So you suggested you arrange the claim, and the handover. Were you still in touch with Sally?'

'Always,' she said. 'Sally was one of my girls. I look after my girls, I always have. She's never been happy, poor Sally, but I did my best for her. So did Malise.'

'So did Brownlow?'

'He's done his best to treat her. But there's always been something there, some weakness – she couldn't cope. I looked after her until she married. I do my best for all my girls, but specially for her, you must believe that. I love Sally like my own child.'

I did believe it, and I was sorry, because I saw that whatever had happened to Jacob would have hurt Sally deeply, and therefore Sandra.

'Did Sally want to meet Jacob?'

'No. It would have hurt her too much. And she thought it would upset him. But I showed her photographs, and she was very proud of him. And when she knew he knew about her, she wanted him to have his rightful money from Malise. He was his son, after all.'

'Are you sure?' I said. 'If Sally was one of your working girls?'

Sandra shook her head violently. 'She wasn't like that. She isn't like that. She was confused, but she never – she wasn't – Malise was the only—'

She stumbled to a stop.

'OK,' I said, to lower the temperature. 'So Jacob decided to take the money. Which was his right. And this was late September, last year?'

'Yes.'

'So from September to early November he waited

in London. For Sally to raise the money? A million in cash is a lot.'

'For Malise to make the arrangements. And Jacob wanted to think, I told you that, to make decisions about his life.'

All that time, he kept out of touch with Jams, I thought. Was it to keep her safe? He could have written, secretly. But Tubbies protected their women: maybe he didn't want to take a risk, however small, because he wouldn't have trusted Sandra. And he was a loner by nature, and perhaps he was savouring his big surprise for her. Look, we're rich.

'Sally gave the money to you to hand over?'

'Into my charge. I used Derek and Dennis.'

'Wasn't that a bit of a risk?'

'Oh, no. They're old friends of mine, very loyal. We were at school together. They've often done little jobs for me, over the years. When friendly persuasion was called for.'

I smiled. She smiled.

'And the handover was where?'

'In London.'

'Where exactly? And who chose it?'

She hesitated, so I prompted her. 'Jacob chose it, didn't he?'

'Yes.'

'Where was it?'

'Most odd,' she said. 'Waste ground, near railway sidings, just west of Paddington. After dark. He insisted it was after dark.'

'And that was when it went wrong,' I said.

Chapter Thirty-Six

'There we are,' said Nanny handing out the last mug, 'nothing beats a nice cup of cocoa.' She left, and closed the door behind her.

We sat in the office and looked at each other. In the corner near the door, Sandra, flanked by Cot and Nappy who were more formally dressed than at our previous meeting, in jeans, boots, cheap shirts and bilious green anoraks. In the corner opposite, Carl, Nick and me. In a third corner, Abraham Master in his security uniform, arms folded and head sunk aggressively on his chest. All of us clutched thick mugs, blue for the boys and pink for the girls, each with our names freshly painted in large black letters. Cot and Nappy's mugs were mostly engulfed by their huge simian paws.

They were drinking the cocoa and their gulps were all that broke the silence. This room was sound-proofed too.

Not such a normal office after all.

'Champion, that,' said Cot, putting his 'Derek' mug down on the desk.

'Ay. I'm reet partial to cocoa,' said Nappy.

Master looked at me. 'You had better have the right,' he said. 'I left my work. And I should be leading evening prayer.'

'Shut your cakehole till summat useful comes out,' snapped Sandra.

I ignored them. 'There are some details you can all help me with, about what happened to Jacob last November.'

Cot and Nappy looked at Sandra. She patted them soothingly. 'I trust her,' she said.

'What about them?' said Cot, jerking his head at Master and Carl.

'Don't worry,' she said.

They settled down.

'Derek and Dennis met him on a railway siding near Paddington, to hand over a very large sum of money,' I went on.

Carl exclaimed in surprise. I looked at him, and he smiled.

I didn't smile back.

'And to get the film,' said Cot. 'The loop, like.'

'Right,' I said. 'Now, I've got to know Jacob quite well, since I've been on his case. I think I understand how his mind worked.'

'That is a privilege reserved to the Lord,' said Master. 'Arrogance is the mark of the beast.'

'He was intelligent, but isolated and supercilious and distrustful. And particularly he wouldn't have trusted Sandra. Not with so much money involved. So he asked for advice from someone who had military training, and experience of security work.'

'That is so,' said Master smugly. 'And I advised him. Meet in an open space. Secure your retreat: have several exits. And take reinforcements.'

'Did you help him choose the place?'

'Yes. He was a civilian. He knew nothing of such matters. I reconnoitred, I chose, and I selected a hide.'

'Did he reconnoitre with you?'

'Yes.'

'Then on the night of the meeting, he took you with him.'

Master clicked impatiently. 'I went ahead, of course. To lay up before the other parties arrived.'

'We didn't see him,' said Cot.

'He worn't there,' said Nappy.

Master looked at them scornfully.

'And maybe you weren't just there as a bodyguard,' I said to him. 'Maybe Jacob was going to pay you the Tubbies' fifty-one per cent share of the million: five hundred and ten thousand pounds. If he was still a Tubby. But his allegiance was wobbling, wasn't it? He'd already abandoned the Tubby teachings on the pleasures of the flesh. He'd lived in the world too long, and his mother was dead. He was going to make a new life.'

'He was studying the work of the first Master. He was searching his heart for the true way,' said Abraham defensively.

Sandra cleared her throat. 'Four hundred and fifty-nine thousand, actually,' she said.

Nick laughed. 'Sandra must have taken ten per cent off the top,' she said to me.

'So good with figures,' said Sandra admiringly to Nick. 'If you want a job, come to me, my dear. On the financial side, of course.'

I went on, talking to Master. 'However, Jacob didn't quite trust you either, did he?'

'My yea is yea and my nay is nay,' he said.

'But they are your own yeas and nays, aren't they? Take this loop copy on the cassette, for example. You told me you didn't know what was on it. I think you did. I think you watched it. And then I think you wiped it, to get rid of the temptation.'

His wet lips wobbled. 'An abomination,' he said.

'Anyway, Jacob didn't quite trust you either. And he was a methodical, obsessive man, who'd ask someone for professional expertise and advice, but would trust his own judgement and make his own plans. So he asked someone else to come along too. His first real friend. Carl.'

Carl shifted in his chair. 'I won't betray his confidence,' he said.

'You told me that before. I don't see why not, since you'd betray anything else,' I said.

'You don't understand,' he said.

'Never mind. So Carl arrived first, and waited, hidden himself and knowing where Master would hide, because it was all planned—'

'I didn't say that,' Carl interrupted.

'And then Master came, and then Jacob met Derek and Dennis. He counted the money, and gave Derek and Dennis the film. What happened then?'

'We went back to the car, didn't we, 'bout three

hundred yards away, it wor. When we got there we heard a noise, so we went back.'

'And now I need to go back quite a way,' I said. 'Master, Jacob didn't go into the Army. Why was that?'

'He had a thin skull,' said Master. 'So the mumbo-jumbo men said, when they x-rayed him as a child. He was healthy but he could not afford injury to the skull. The Lord had decreed it so.'

'So any blow to the head could kill him. And you knew that. And when you fought with him for your share of the money, and you hit him, you knew that.'

'He was in the hands of the Lord. And I fought not for my share, but for the church's share.'

'What could the Tubbies do with half a million pounds?' said Sandra.

'The work of the Lord,' said Master.

'And it wouldn't hurt your chances with the girl from the chippy, either,' I said.

He glared at me.

I looked at Cot and Nappy. 'Was Jacob alive when you got back to him?' I said.

They looked at Sandra. She nodded. 'No. He wor dead, and the money gone,' Cot said. 'Messy, like. We couldn't leave a mess for Sandra, so we took him home.'

'And put the body where?'

'Some of uz mates wor pouring concrete on the M18 extension. We popped him in there. Donny's got a reet good motorway system. Thirty minutes to Hull.'

'Twenty-five minutes to Sheffield. Champion,' said Nappy.

'Meanwhile Master had taken the money and run away.'

'I extracted from an untenable position,' said Master pompously.

Cot snorted. 'We were shit-scared an' all, but at least we cleared up uz mess,' he said.

'And Master ran away from Derek and Dennis, presumably,' I said.

'I made a tactical withdrawal, yes.'

'And you ran into Carl.'

'I never—' began Carl.

'Do shut up,' said Sandra. 'Never met such a big girl's blouse.'

'I don't know who I ran into,' said Master. 'I was hit from behind, and knocked unconscious.' He sounded embarrassed. 'When I recovered, the money had gone. I looked for it, obviously, but—'

'But Carl had taken it. In Jacob's holdall. The holdall I searched in his room in Chicago.'

'That was empty,' Carl said.

'Not quite. It had a small round black plastic disc in it.' I fished something out of my pocket and held it on my palm to show him. 'Like this one.'

'A button,' said Carl.

'No. You switched it for a button. And I'd never seen it but I'd felt it, and my fingers remembered it wasn't a button. It doesn't have holes, but it has raised writing on it, which says *Haig Fund*.'

'What the hell does that mean?' said Carl.

Cot and Nappy got up and moved to stand in front of the door.

'In November is Remembrance Day. A big com-
memoration of all the fighting men who've died for
Britain. And for two weeks before, the Haig Fund col-
lects money for ex-servicemen. You give money, they
give you a poppy to wear to show you've contributed.
A red nylon flower with a black plastic centre, like
this. Half the adult population of this country wear
poppies. Especially Tubbies or ex-Tubbies, to show
respect to the generation they lost in the First World
War. "In Flanders fields the poppies blow/ Between
the crosses, row on row". '

'That's crap,' said Carl.

Nappy crossed the room faster than I would have
thought possible for him, though it still wasn't very
fast, picked Carl up and hit him on the nose. 'That's
poetry,' he said, 'and it's champion.'

Then he dropped Carl back into his chair and
returned to the door.

I went on. 'Jacob was wearing a poppy. And in the
struggle with Master the flower part must have torn
and the centre fell into the holdall. Where I found it.'

Carl put his hand on my arm. I pulled my arm
away. 'Hey,' he said. 'Hey, Alex—'

I looked at Sandra. 'I'm handing Carl over to you,' I
said. 'Ninety per cent of what you recover goes to
Jams.'

'Of course, dear,' she said confidently. 'We'll sort it.'

'What about the church's share?' said Master.

'You killed him. Be grateful I'm not handing you
over to the police,' I said. 'Don't expect money too.'

'Forgiveness is the Lord's,' said Master. 'I have faith in his mercy. I will discuss it with Emily Treliving.'

'Alex, I thought we were really close,' said Carl. 'Look at me.'

I looked at him. He had wonderful hair, terrific skin and eyes like the young Robert Mitchum. 'Abroad doesn't count,' I said.

'What? What do you mean?'

'Plus Jacob trusted you. He took you along as back-up, to protect him. You did nothing, and he was killed, and you stole his money. You're a coward and a thief. Come on, Nick.'

We crossed to the door. I opened it. Nanny was standing in the doorway. 'I've come for the mugs,' she said brightly.

Carl hurled his mug at a filing cabinet and made a dash for the door. Nappy caught him and tossed him to Cot, who wrapped his arms around him and held him, kicking, clear of the floor.

'Careless,' said Nanny, 'you've broken your nice mug. Shall I come back later, Sandra?'

'Do,' said Sandra warmly. 'We're just going to have a friendly chat with a naughty boy.'

'Help,' Carl shouted. 'Help.'

'Temper, temper. There'll be tears before bedtime,' said Nanny.

Chapter Thirty-Seven

I was still in the bath at half-past seven, when Polly came in. I'd been soaking for thirty-five minutes and I was wrinkling like a prune.

'You've been in there too long,' said Polly. 'Get out this minute.' She looked tired and cross, and old, for her. She closed the lavatory seat and slumped down on it. 'D'you want a takeaway, this evening? We could watch *Death in Venice*.'

That was a sop: she didn't like the film, I did. 'Sorry,' I said. 'I'm having a Very Significant Dinner with Barty.'

'Oh,' she said, life stirring. 'What are you going to wear?'

'The outfit you brought me from Hong Kong,' I said.

'The Donna Karan? Yes, that'll do, but it's a bit informal, where are you going?'

'Alberto's.'

'Fine for Alberto's . . . Tell you what, I've got some great shoes – are you going to marry him? No, don't tell me, he should be the first to know, he'll be so happy—'

'Towel, please,' I said.

She passed me a towel. 'Come downstairs, I'll do your face.'

'Do it up here.'

'With this?' she said, peering contemptuously at the sparse contents of my small make-up bag. 'Did Michelangelo paint with four crayons?'

'I don't know, did he?'

'That outfit needs earrings. And bracelets, I think.'

'Not bracelets. They always catch on things, when I wear them.'

'What things?'

'Plants. Tables. Waiters.'

'I'm going down. You'd better follow me,' she said. 'Now.'

We both looked at my face in her mirror. Michelangelo couldn't have done a better job, I had to admit. I wished she'd do her own, next, and stop looking so unhappy.

'Is it Magnus?' I said.

'Yes. He's perfect.'

'He is rather.'

'I can't bear him,' she said. 'And I can't bear not bearing him. And if I have to go round one more perfect house I'll spit.'

'Has it occurred to you that he's gay?'

She met my eyes in the mirror. 'Gay?' she said, horrified. 'Why?'

'Barty and Nick and Grace all think so. Because of his response to the film this morning.'

'Gay,' she said. 'The film? What about it? I thought his manner was a bit off, actually.'

'Probably put on to cover his interest in Big Dick Tracy.'

'I didn't notice.'

'They did. I wasn't there.'

'Gay,' she said thoughtfully. 'If he's gay he's not perfect, is he? Not as a husband, I mean, though he'd be perfect for another gay, of course, if he came out of the closet, that is. Which means . . .'

She was smiling.

'Which means you can keep on bonking your boss,' I said briskly.

She blushed. 'Richard,' she said.

'If that's his name.'

'I *told* you.'

'So you did. The married misunderstood bald one. You didn't tell me you were bonking him, however.'

'I wish you wouldn't use that word,' she said. 'And I didn't tell you because I thought you'd be cross, and how do you know he's bald?'

I started to laugh. Soon, so did she.

'Lovely wine,' I said.

'Good,' said Barty. 'As this is a special occasion, I won't tell you what it is.'

He seemed relaxed. Pleasantly tired, perhaps, after Grace. We had a good table, tucked away in a corner at the front, not too close to the other tables and with a good view of the street through the wide window.

'Case wrapped up?' he said, when we'd ordered.

I explained, very briefly. He nodded, unsurprised. 'Clever of you to spot the poppy clue,' he said. 'I'd no idea that anything was written on the black bit in the middle.'

'Whatever that black thing in the holdall was, it wasn't a poppy middle. It was perfectly smooth. The point was, he'd switched it. Looking back, I was sure he'd switched it, whatever it was. Nothing, I expect. But it's the sort of spurious evidence that shakes your nerve if you're guilty.'

He laughed. 'Was Nick pleased?'

'Very. She didn't like him.'

'Where is she now?'

'Spending the evening with Grace,' I said.

Silence. I watched the street and thought about Jams. I hadn't told her yet. Tomorrow would be soon enough.

Barty coughed. He was beginning to look tense. This was up to me. 'I've been thinking. About what you said. And I agree with some of it, I am selfish and narrow and ungiving. Some of the time. But I've always been that, and you picked me, I didn't pick you. So it must suit you somehow.'

'It did,' he said. 'You're right. It did.'

'But less now?'

'Less now.'

I fished down my bra for the list I'd made the

night before. 'So you want to share your feelings with me?'

'I suppose so,' he said, looking slightly appalled. 'What's that?'

'A list of the things you said to Polly last night.'

'I was rather drunk, last night.'

'In Ancient Rome, if you committed a crime when you were drunk you were punished twice. Once for the crime, once for being drunk.'

'I didn't know that.'

'So I'm ignorant, huh?' I said.

'Are you going to marry me or not?' he said. He sounded half-serious, half-amused.

'I have to share your feelings, first,' I said.

'Another put-off,' he said angrily.

I put my hand out to take his reassuringly. At that moment our first course arrived and the hand I took was the waiter's.

When we'd sorted it out and the waiter'd gone, the moment had passed, but Barty wasn't angry any more. 'It isn't another put-off,' I said. 'It's a good point. You say you want to marry me, but there's all these things you haven't told me about.'

'Because you haven't asked.'

'I'm asking now.'

'What are you asking?'

I glanced down the list:

mother
grandmother
childhood

dog who died
first time he knew he loved me
where live
emeralds
Comme des Garçons
friend's production company
hinterlands
the meaning of life

I read it twice, and thought. Mostly I thought about why I felt so paralysingly shy.

'Alex,' he said, 'are you doing this to hurt me?'

'No. Really not. It's – loops.'

'Loops?'

'Little toy-train circles, that everyone chugs round. Like Jacob. Obsessive. Had to know best. Didn't trust anyone, so loneliness made him trust the wrong person.'

'Only fifty per cent of the time,' said Barty. 'He was right to trust Jams.'

'I suppose . . . But that was luck. Anyway, I think you want me to leave my loop. I can't leave it, but I could broaden it. Put in branch lines, you know. And I'm trying, but it's hard. So I make a list because I like lists and I make a sort of joke because it's safer.'

'You're very honest,' he said. 'That's one of the reasons I love you so much. Will you let me see the list?'

'No. OK, I'm ready to start. We'll start with – the dog you had, that died.'

'Why start there?' he said tenderly.

I hesitated. But he'd said he liked my honesty, hadn't he? 'It's probably the dullest,' I said. 'We can get it over with.'